The Leap Year

by

The Contemporary Women

Writers' Club

Grosvenor House
Publishing Limited

For more information about
The Contemporary Women Writers' Club visit
www.queenbee.co.uk

This book is published by
Grosvenor House Publishing Ltd
28-30 High Street, Guildford, Surrey, GU1 3HY.
www.grosvenorhousepublishing.co.uk

A CIP record for this book
is available from the British Library

ISBN 978-1-907211-15-7

About

The Leap Year is the first collection from *The Contemporary Women Writers' Club*. We are six British-based writers, some established, others emerging, who meet regularly around our kitchen tables to discuss new ideas and approaches to our fiction.

The Leap Year challenges contemporary publishing conventions. It has been independently conceived, created, printed and distributed, yet with the same rigorous attention to detail, quality and finish as any commercially-published title. The internet makes the book global, a neat reflection of the stories conjured within its pages, which cover every continent.

The anthology charts transformational moments in twelve women's lives over the consecutive months of a year. Each story is set in a different country and considers a particular life stage. The 'leaps' in the book are often physical or emotional – and always psychological. Common themes recur: self-recognition, re-evaluation and reinvention.

All members of *The Contemporary Women Writers' Club* share a desire to write and to keep writing, to publish and keep publishing. Through our new imprint, Queenbee Press, we intend to do just that – and so celebrate and perpetuate the art of quality women's fiction.

Lucy Cavendish, Miranda Glover, Rachel Jackson,
Alexa Hughes Wilson, Anne Tuite-Dalton and Jennie Walmsley.

Introduction
by Kathy Lette

This is a book about journeys. (Have globe – will trot.) Of course a woman's favourite destination is a cosy little spot which goes by the name of G. (Boys, do please set off on a sexual safari with a list of edible berries and a compass. It will be so worth it.) But it's not just physical journeys encapsulated in this impressive collection, but emotional, spiritual and psychological ones too.

If book groups were the buzzword of the last decade (when did buzzword become a buzzword by the way?) then creative writing groups are the next logical step. The six authors in this collection met as harassed mums. (Harassed mothers? Surely a tautology?) Tired of living vicariously through the novels they read at home or in their book clubs, they decided to put pun to paper by writing their own stories. I suppose the best analogy is that of a group of women meeting to discuss recipes, but then deciding to cook their own - with some very delectable results.

These remarkable women then set about building their own kitchen – in this case, a publishing house, Queenbee Press, in order to see their own work in print. The best thing about being a writer is that it doesn't involve any heavy lifting. You can also drink heavily on the job, work in your jammies all day and have affairs and call it research. And, as I'm sure the authors now know, it's also much, much cheaper than therapy.

Women dream of being taken somewhere exotic. (Although being taken standing up backwards by Brad Pitt would also suffice.) But we are usually just taken for granted, for a ride, or to the cleaners when hubby leaves you for a younger woman. This book is your literary cure. Administer immediately. And fasten your psychological seat belt for a very exciting ride.

Acknowledgements

Thanks are due to those who have helped us to work together on this collection – our partners, our children and our friends. A heartfelt thanks to Lindsay and David Chesterton for their generous loan of Boussac, without which this anthology would never have come into being. Thank you Kathy Lette for your introduction, Charles Glover for photography and Michael Agar for design. Thank you Lara Daniels for copy editing, Russell Amerasekera for your creative advice, Sarah Allen for jumping in, Truffle for surviving the wheels of the truck and, of course, Lisa for making the leap.

Contents
The Leap Year

January | Argentina
Lucy Cavendish

At first she wasn't sure. The shimmering heat outside bleached everything white and the sudden cool darkness of the cattle barn made her head feel hazy. But still, eventually, once her sight had cleared, Consuela saw her, lying prostrate like an abandoned mannequin at the back of the barn, head simply touching the remains of last year's dry straw fodder. Her arms were limply lying out by her sides, like a bird that had fallen to earth.Consuela recognised that pallid skin, so white it always looked as if someone had blown powder over her. And that hair, that burnished hair, the same colour as the pampas when the sun has burned it dry and then the rain has streaked red earthy mud into it. It clung damply to one naked shoulder.

Consuela walked towards her.
"Senora Carolina," she said tentatively.
She screwed her eyes up to try and see more in the dim light. The body was not moving.
"Senora Carolina," she said more loudly. *"Esta usted bien?"*
There was no reply. Consuela crept forward, putting one old silent crepe-clad foot in front of the other. There was a smell. Consuela stopped. What was it? It reminded her of something, something acrid. It stung her nose. She just couldn't remember what it was. Then, suddenly, a shaft of sunlight came through the roof of the barn and shone on the body directly. Consuela gasped and gave out a scream. Her hand flew to the crucifix around her neck.
"Mi dios!"
She stood transfixed. Then, almost imperceptibly crossing herself, she went towards the body. It was her. La mujer del jefe and she was covered in blood.

At seven o'clock in the morning Carolina de Avendano got up, fastened her silk nightgown around her thin body and went into the next bedroom. Eduardo was lying in bed in exactly the same position as he had been when he fell asleep last night. His dark haired nurse, Felicia, jolted awake when she heard the door close. She opened her eyes blearily.

"*Buenos dias,*" said Carolina, slightly sharply.

Felicia stifled a yawn and rubbed her eyes, trying to open them, as a child would.

"*Buen' dia,*" she replied in a faltering voice.

She made no move to get up from her chair so Carolina strode to open the large windows and pushed back the wooden shutters that kept the room as dark as night, even when the midday sun was at its most fierce. The light poured in, like a volcano erupting into the room. Carolina noticed a small whiff of dust. Didn't anyone ever dust the room?

She turned to look at Felicia but found the nurse was looking down, sheltering her eyes from the sudden sunlight by concentrating on rearranging her skirts. She was going to ask her why she never dusted the shutters but then the thought occurred to her that maybe it wasn't in Felicia's job brief to do so. Did nurses dust? Were they like the nannies she had as a child in England, responsible for all duties relating to the children? Or were they only responsible for the medical side of things? The taking of the pills? The removal of bed pans? Carolina knew Felicia did more than that. She had spied her many a time stroking Eduardo's hair back from his face, washing his chest with a cool flannel. Sometimes Carolina would find Felicia sitting on the bed crooning folk songs to him, holding his hand in hers and saying sadly, 'pobre cito, Senor Eduardo' and then, when she would catch Carolina looking at her, she'd drop his hand and lower her eyes. There is defiance there though. That Carolina does know.

Carolina turned to look out of the windows. Eduardo's room was at the front of the estancia. Of course he had the best bedroom, with the windows that led on to the verandah that ran along the entire first floor of the ranch house. He had chosen this room years ago when he had first brought his bride over from her home to this foreign and strange country. This was long before the accident that had him laid out and motionless on his oak bed. They were young then, she was just twenty-four years old, him a few years more. How could she have known that merely three decades later her husband would be stretched out, half dead, on a bed that she hadn't shared with him for years.

Carolina had always liked this room, even though her own bedroom was at the back of the house, much darker but, then again, much cooler. No vista for her though. All she saw every morning were the barns and the herd of beef cattle that seemed to live forever in their repetitive small world. Sometimes Carolina would watch them go through their endlessly dull daily routine and think, 'do animals get déjà vu?' Every time they came in to be jabbed, checked, killed, did they think 'have I been here before?' Or were they like goldfish, endlessly doing the same thing but forgetting every rotation round the fish bowl? Every day Carolina watched the cattle eat, defecate and then eat more. Sometimes, when there was to be a killing, she'd hear the cattle get restless. They'd moan and groan as one of the herd would be taken to the very back of the barn where the long sharp knives hung. Carolina hated the noise. She'd shut her windows, close her shutters, put her head under the pillow. Carolina knows that animals scream. It's just that very few other people ever hear it.

Eduardo had the view of the polo ponies. Before he became totally immobile, before the frayed nerves of his spine totally gave in to the myriad unstable fractures in them, Carolina used to wheel him out on to the verandah so he could watch his beloved string doze and graze and then, sometimes, get the wind in their tails and rush about the fields kicking and whinnying in excitement. Sometimes they behaved like children. The young ones – Cielo, Poquito and Madrigal – would pretend-fight and the older ones neigh. Carolina watched Eduardo then, when the horses were at their most playful. She could see his eyes light up.
"They are like you Eduardo,' she'd say, 'Little children who want to have fun but can't wipe their own bottoms."

The sun was already burning down on the backs of the ponies out in the fields. Carolina could see them there, huddled in the shelters already, flicking their tails and shaking their heads trying to get rid of the flies. Was it Diablo standing there, separate from the other ones? Carolina squinted. Yes, she could see him now, that small black horse with his one white sock. He had his ears back, teeth slightly bared. God, that animal didn't like anything. Suddenly, Carolina had an image of Eduardo on Diablo, crashing down against the far post of the polo pitch, his head and back landing on the post with a sickening thump and Diablo standing there, still like now, teeth bared, eyes bright.

"I see Diablo," Carolina said, turning casually towards her husband.

Eduardo's eyes flickered towards her.

"Yes, Diablo. He's standing in the sun and it's so hot out there Eduardo." Eduardo's eyes moved again.

"Well, I could go and move him into the pony barn I suppose," said Carolina letting her finger trail down the cool of the window, "but... I am busy. The estancia won't run itself and, as you can't help, I'll have to get on with it by myself."

Eduardo's eyes looked away and towards Felicia.

"You think Felicia..." Carolina arched an eyebrow towards the nurse. Then she went to the bed and sat on it, up close to her husband's lifeless body. "You listen to me Eduardo," she whispered almost as a caress, her lips close to his ear. "Everything will be lost here. Do you understand?" Eduardo looked at her and then back towards the window.

"No," said Carolina as she got up. "I won't do it for you. If Pàmela was here, or Juanita or maybe Gaelle or....who else Eduardo? Who else loves you enough to move your precious pony, your caballo especial? Felicia?" Felicia looked at Carolina uncomprehendingly when she heard her name. Carolina gave a tinkly laugh.

"No Eduardo. She can't handle Diablo. She's a nurse not a caballera. Try asking someone else."

Then Carolina left the room.

Half an hour later, Carolina was dressed and sitting down at the long table in the dining room. Nothing had changed in this room. It seemed exactly the same as when Carolina had first come here as a young bride, all those years ago. Back then, going to an estancia many hours drive away from Buenos Aires felt as if she was setting off on a different part of her life. There was nothing here then. No telephones, no electricity, no shops. Computers, the internet, the worldwide web were years away from being invented. Yet, even though now everything in the world had changed, here, here in this heat, this dust, still no telephone rang, no fax buzzed through, no computer hummed. Eduardo just wouldn't have it. For a long time Carolina wondered why her husband had bucked the trends of time. As the rest of the world became accessible, as people as far and wide as Kinshasha, Woolangong and Fife twittered away to each other twenty-four hours a day, she sat in silence. She used to think that Eduardo desired to be unobtainable, that somehow, if he did not have peace here in this estancia, he would have peace nowhere. Now she thinks it was because he wanted her to be unobtainable, cut off, silent, stuck and somehow she too had become wary of letting the outside world in.

On this morning she had, as was her habit, made an effort to stick to the routine her husband had put in place many years ago: always dress for breakfast. Always have breakfast at 8am. How many times had Carolina done this? Got up, dressed in long fawn riding trousers, a crisply laundered white long-sleeved shirt, a handkerchief tied round her neck, a hat ready for her head. How many times had she sat at this long dark table clad for action but left alone? When she was first married, it hadn't been like that. Eduardo would always be at the table before her. He would motion for her to sit down next to him, not right at the other end. He would cup her face in his hands and kiss her and then turn back to the newspapers. He was always full of news himself – how the Chief of Police in Buenos Aires had lost his lover, how the wife of the Deputy had run off with a high-ranking member of the military. He knew everyone of course. They all revolved around each other, constantly jostling each other off polo ponies at the Army pitch. He would skip over everything else.
"Politics leaves me cold!" he'd say, taking a hearty swig of coffee before jumping up and going to see how his horses were. Back then, Carolina didn't care about what was happening in her adopted homeland. What did she know of the missing? Of the junta? Of the disappeared sons and grieving mothers? All she knew was that she was here because she was in love.

But what had being here taught her? That her fair English skin would never tan? That she was made from thin frail paper, from her skin right through to her heart? That however long she stayed in the god-forsaken, fly-blown estancia, she would never be healthy? She had coughed every

7

day since she got here. It was driving her insane. Sometimes she longed for the damp wetness of Shropshire – strangely, she coughed less at home or was that just her fading memory – and the smell of her mother's long-dead, shaggy, old rain-soaked labrador who would sleep with her as a child and who her father fed from his own plate.

"Pup loves cook's macaroni cheese," he'd say as the dog would gratefully lap away at the spoon, its little moist pink tongue darting in and out.

In a way, once she was older, she'd found it revolting. She remembered how embarrassing she found it when Eduardo came to stay at Chullington for the only time.

"*El perro siempre comer del plato de su padre?*" Eduardo had said to her, raising his eyebrows.

The only thing she can remember is her mother saying, "I am afraid we don't speak Spanish," to Eduardo in a very slow voice as if speaking to a child.

Eduardo had left the table then.

"I can speak English perfectly well Lady Cutliffe," he said to himself. They never returned to Chullington after that.

No, now she couldn't see the difference between that life and this. She thought the endless silence, the cold room, the lack of anyone there who actually said anything would drive her mad if she remained at Chullington. But she'd swapped it for something pretty much the same, she just hadn't known it at the time.

This morning, she had rung the bell twice but still Consuela had not appeared. Carolina was reading the papers, a half-eaten boiled egg pushed to one side. She wanted Consuela to come and clear the table but...Carolina sighed. She got up, took the plate in her hand and carried it to the kitchen. It was empty. The back door was open. There were fly nets on the windows. She pushed a strand of strawberry-coloured hair back from her forehead. Already she was sweating. She could feel the small patches of damp seeping through the crispness of her shirt. Three flies were buzzing round next to the sink, frantically bashing backwards and forwards against the nets; their mad attempt to get out. Another few were hovering over the bin as Carolina turned to put her egg shell in it. She noticed a ball of dough sitting on the worktop, wrapped in muslin. A pot was on the cooker, gently steaming under a lid. Carolina took the lid off and inhaled. The familiar smell of rosemary, thyme and peppermint seeped in to her nostrils. Carolina took a step back. She had smelled this particular mix of herbs almost too often over the years. Why was Consuela boiling up herbs for a poultice?

Just then, a shadow appeared on the whitewashed wall of the pony stall opposite the house. Angelo was leading a meek and mild but definitely limping Diablo. Every so often, as they passed, the man would turn and talk to the horse, putting his lips against the flattened ears, running one splayed hand down Diablo's neck, as if that hand alone with its strength and breadth could contain the spirit of the horse, preventing him from skittering and making the hurt leg so much worse.

"El es muy bueno con caballos," said a voice from behind Carolina. It was so unexpected, it made her jump. She turned to see Consuela.

"Es Angelo," said Consuela proudly.

She went to reach for the felt to start making the poultice.

"I'll do it,' said Carolina, suddenly. The sharpness of her voice sounded strange even to her. "I mean, I'll make it up and take it out to Angelo. OK?" She smiled at Consuela. Consuela smiled back at her.

"Si Senora Carolina. Lo que usted desea." Whatever you desire.

Consuela had asked Carolina some months ago if her nephew could come and work here for a short period of time. She had told her he could work the ranch for her and, God knows, Carolina needed someone. Her own son Eduardo had been lost to her for some time now. He was in Buenos Aires trying to organise the mothers of the lost, the Asociacion Madres de Plaza de Mayo, but it was hopeless. The junta had left a long time ago and now no one paraded outside the Casa Rosada any more. But still Eduardo Junior sat at his desk and filed his papers, filing away those memories of a father too involved with polo and women and not involved enough with his son. But no one really noticed anymore because he wasn't a mother and he hadn't lost anyone at all. Only me, thought Carolina. For years she had tried to breach the gap with her first born but, in his own vague way, he had remained out of her reach and away from everything that reminded him of home. He was not at all like Angelo. This is what had struck Carolina on meeting Consuela's nephew when he came to see her. Where Eduardo Junior was tall and thin like a strand of malnourished pale grass that lingered at the edge of the pampas, Angelo was broad, tanned, stocky. Where Eduardo junior paid his father back by loudly insisting he was terrified of horses, Angelo moved quietly amongst the herd as if he were part of it.

Consuela had brought him in to meet her one afternoon. Carolina had been having tea in the drawing room, sipping on her cup of Earl Grey and eating the corner off a small piece of Scottish shortbread that her daughter brought her every time she visited from Buenos Aires. Feeding time at the zoo Carolina would think when her slightly overweight yet expensively well-maintained daughter would get out of her Grand Cherokee weighed down with 'gifts' for her mother. Since when had Carolina wanted 85% cocoa chocolate, pats of slightly melted organic butter, huge hunks of parmesan from the Italian deli in Palermo? But the shortbread? She had to admit she liked that.

She always wondered if these trips were a sop to her. Her daughter and her children obviously hated being here. When they were younger, the children liked to ride the ponies bareback across the field. Now they whined on about how abuela had no computer, no Nintendo Wii, no plasma television. They were not interested in the comings and goings of the chickens, the cows, the beef herd. They did not want to see the cicadas singing in the pampas, the birds skimming over the stream. They made Carolina feel almost relieved to be here and not in their whirring world of computer warfare.

Sometimes Carolina would sigh when they'd gone. Her daughter bored her solidly about the latest Buenos Aires party she had attended and how her low-ranking military husband Jorge had paid for her to get an infinity rainfall shower installed in their en-suite. Sometimes, when they'd gone, Carolina walked out onto the estancia and breathed in the heavy evening air. She'd wonder what would become of her – stuck here in a place that was falling down around her, a place she could not maintain or manage. How could she leave? Where would she go? It was obvious a life with her daughter in Buenos Aires would not be an option for her and the money was running out, no doubt about that.

One night, as she had sat in the kitchen and poured herself a glass of cool home-made lemonade, Angelo had appeared at the back door, his face half-obscured by the fly net. She had jumped when she saw him, her hands flying to her neck. He had said nothing.

"Tu quieres algo,"' she asked him. Do you want something?

He motioned towards the jug. Carolina had opened the door for him and he had wordlessly come in and slowly drunk a glass of lemonade, his throat heaving gently, and then left.

Somehow, of an evening, after Consuela had gone upstairs to turn down Carolina's bed, this had become a routine. Carolina would sit in the half light waiting for Angelo to come in and drink lemonade. Sometimes he just sat at the table and closed his eyes and Carolina sat there too, quietly watching him. She liked doing this, she realised. His quiet presence reassured her. She was, maybe, a bit like Diablo after all.

Carolina went to the cow barn, still carrying the poultice for Diablo's hurt leg. She had looked for Angelo in the pony stalls but found only Diablo standing there and rolling his eyes. She had called out Angelo's name for the first time ever but there had been no reply, only the sound of the horse chomping on some dry strands of hay. And then she remembered. It was the first Tuesday of the month, the killing day, the day when a chosen member of the beef herd was slaughtered. She made her way to the barn and saw him, shirtless, his muscles standing out, his body wet and shiny like a piece of polished mahogany. She stopped, transfixed, at the door of the cow barn, her tongue moist in her mouth as she watched him straddle the cow and swiftly bring its head back. The cow attempted to buck in a futile fashion, straining its neck as Angelo yanked the head back further, forcing the animal to reveal its main artery to the world. There it was, pulsating and vibrant, the blood running through it now, but soon... just one sweeping movement and it would be dead, the life pumping out of it.

The cow seemed to sense this. It struggled and pushed against Angelo's soaked and sweating chest.

"Escuchame," Angelo said to the cow harshly as he wrenched its head to one side then the other. *"Todo tiene que morir. Asi es como es."*

Carolina gasped as the cow opened its mouth to bellow and, just as it did, Angelo flashed the knife back and swept it across the underside of the beast's neck. The blood seeped out in a thin red line, as if the wound was somehow surprised that it had been opened. As Angelo turned to lay the heaving animal's head on the ground, its blood began to flow faster and faster, gushing now over Angelo's hands, splashing up onto his chest. Carolina felt as if she was going to faint.

"Excuse me," she said quietly as the ground seemed to move up towards her. Oh Christ. She really was going to faint. She closed her eyes, hoping to steady herself, and reached out hoping to find the coolness of the barn wall. Instead she found something warm and almost clammy in front of her. "Carolina," said Angelo as she clung onto his arms. She held onto him, clutching at him. She breathed in deeply.

'Lo siento Angelo,' she said, her arms still grasping him. "I'm so sorry, it's just that I, I..."

She could feel his arms around her now, round her back, underneath her shirt, on her skin. He was holding her up against him, supporting her frailty with his torso. She sunk into him. She could smell him now, such a raw smell. She knew it so well. She smelled it every slaughter day when the blood was fresh, before it dried out and stunk and became encrusted with flies. Strange how blood smells of what it is, she thought, her head still spinning. When something is dead and gone and dried, the insects come and make it putrid. But when it is fresh, it is almost alive. I wonder if I lick it, if I lick this cow's blood, will it taste of grass and iron and all the things the cow loved. Will it still taste of the fur of the calf this cow once gave birth to? Will it taste of joy and happiness or loss and sorrow and sadness? Carolina wondered what her own blood would taste of. She knows the answer. It would taste of sorrow.

Carolina didn't know what came over her. All she knew was that if she stuck out her tongue and gently licked at this body in front of her, she would find the answer to everything. So she gently touched her tongue against Angelo's chest. How did this man taste? Bitter, salty, ferrous. Angelo gasped when he felt her. She could feel him take a sharp breath in and then, suddenly, he lifted her up in his arms as if she weighed no more than a small child and carried her over to the back of the barn where the hay and straw lay in heaps on the ground.

Her eyes were still shut. She loved the sensation of her feet trailing in the blood seeping across the barn. She felt her shirt being pulled up and over her head as her arms went up to help. Her crisp ironed trousers being pulled down from her pale hips, her knickers following them down her body, usually so cold and thin and dry but now seemingly alive with a snail's trail of blood down it as Angelo's mouth followed the movement of her underwear. Then she could feel his mouth on her nipples. He tugged at them with his teeth, just as a baby would. It made her tingle. For a moment she remembered Eduardo Junior nestling there as a baby with his black hair looking just like his father, sucking away insistently. What had been the point of all that love, she thought suddenly? Why had she sat with her lace nightgown pulled to one side so that he could have access to her? How had he repaid her? How had any of them repaid her?

Carolina suddenly felt an anger so violent it propelled her back to that nursery – her own nursery of no love or joy, just endless scoldings from austere governesses who could not understand why she coughed. Then the nursery here in this estancia, so hot she could not keep those babies cool even though she wrapped wet cold flannels on their foreheads. She would watch them as they lay there like patients listening to their mother read to them. Yet she knew they were stuck there, all three of them, in the strange web Eduardo had woven to keep them captured and unable to leave the endless buzzing, buzzing, buzzing of those flies. Was something buzzing now? Her head, so full of thoughts. She didn't want to think.

She opened her eyes, slightly disorientated, to see Angelo before her, kneeling up now in front of her, his brown hands on her white thighs, now moving towards her jutting out hips, pulling her towards him. He leaned over her and kissed her, deep and long, and she thought her head would explode. This is the buzzing she thought as Angelo took his lips away and moved back to look at her.

She marvelled at him, not a boy, not a child, but a man with rough skin on his hands. She moved towards him but he pulled away from her again and took her left hand. She watched him as he pulled it towards him, opening up her palm and then stroking it slowly and deliberately down her own body, daubing a trail of blood as it went. He then dropped her hand limply to the side and took his own hand to her legs, pushing his fingers between her thighs and inside her, moving his fingers insistently and deliciously as he stared at her face, and moved them in and out of her, faster now. Then, suddenly, he stopped. She closed her eyes and faintly smiled.

"Again," she said, proffering her right hand.

He took it to the floor and trailed it in the pool of blood that was slowly forming around them. Then he stroked that hand down her body, abandoning it as he sunk his fingers back into her.

"Jesus Christ," she said as she began to rock back and forth on them. Her hands reached forwards and felt for the zipper on his trousers. He had a belt on. She couldn't undo it. He stopped his rhythmic fingers and started to undo it. She sat up and watched him hazily as he stood up and let his rough work trousers fall to the ground. He looked like a God, a priapic God ready for his sacrifice of blood and ashes.

Carolina licked her lips and fell back, opening her legs wide to him.

"Take it," she said. "It has been too long. Just take it."

Angelo looked at her and then sunk into her.

"It's been so long," she said again into his black oiled hair. She arched her back. Had he heard her? It was important to her that he had.

"I said, take it Angelo," she said again, thrumming her fingers on to his back and letting out a moan.

"Fucking take it Angelo. Take it!"

He raised his head up and looked at her.

"Not me," she said, gasping not sure if he'd understood. "You've already taken me. You are taking me now."

Angelo began to move fiercely in and out of her once more, responding to her hands on his rump insisting he move faster, quicker, harder.

"No, not just me. Todos. Everything."

She let out a small scream as he bent towards her to kiss her. She bit him sharply on the lip and licked his blood off before he could rear back. He stared at her.

"The estancia Angelo," she said, her eyes shut now. 'It's yours. The land, the cows, the horses, Diablo, Eduardo, Felicia. The whole bloody lot.

"Take it Angelo," she said. "Take it. Take it. Take it."

By the time the police came, the body had gone.

Consuela couldn't understand it. She told the police she had been there, la mujer del jefe, in the back of the barn.

"Donde esta la cuerpo ahora?" joked the officer with the black waxed moustache. "Where your body now, little cooking lady?" he said, raising his eyebrows at his younger companions.

"Pero habia sangre. Yo lo vi," said Consuela, almost crying now.

"You saw blood?" said the officer. "Of course you did! The blood of the cow. We came for the murder of the lady, not the bloody cow."

Later on, once they had poked around the barn, once they had finally persuaded Consuela that the mujer del jefe was not lying there bloodied and dead, they went to talk to Angelo. Maybe he knows something, Consuela told them. They found him alone in the kitchen, sipping a glass of cool lemonade, smiling.

"Ha ido," he said to the policemen when they asked him of the whereabouts of Senora Carolina.

'Gone where?' they said to him, but Angelo just shrugged.

"No lo se," he said. I don't know.

After the police had left, Angelo got up to lock the back door. One fly was still left, buzzing away at the net. Angelo looked at it for a second and then, almost casually, squashed it with his fingers.

February | Montreal
Anne Tuite-Dalton

A cold wind, carrying flakes of snow, whirls into the lobby when I open the door. I shiver and tighten the belt of Jo's black coat. She bought it only last year for a recital of Bach's St Matthew's Passion. Her choir had given a performance outside the St Denis theatre. Stepping out, I scan the road for Henry's car; it's parked a few yards away. I come down carefully, the last step has disappeared under the snow and my foot sinks into the thick whiteness. Henry is there now, I take his arm and relax. We say hello but around us all is quiet, muffled, the silence seems to suit our mood and we hold onto our thoughts in the car.

We are the first to arrive. The crematorium is a small modern church and thankfully warm. I sit down at the front, on the right hand side, Henry beside me. In the past few months he has been supportive, driving me to hospital, comforting me when I argued with the consultants over Jo's treatment, cajoling the nurses so they took extra care of their patient. Now I long to be on my own, with her absence as my only companion.

I hear commotion. I try to concentrate, look down at my hands. She used to kiss them, say how beautiful they were. Now they are frail, the veins visible, three-dimensional, and my skin is marked with dots of different sizes and varying shades of brown. I strain to focus and to remember her hands, so different, smaller and fleshier, always soft.

The constant opening and closing of the door and the hushed voices bring me back to the present. People are arriving. Though I don't turn around – I will see them soon enough, they are coming back to the flat for drinks and something to eat afterwards – I cannot help it, I imagine them: Jo's colleagues, looking like typical librarians in their fleeces and comfy shoes; some of our neighbours; the girl I see at swimming every week with her short cropped hair and beautiful features; the lovely

Jamaican nurse, Darling, who looked after Jo so well in hospital, bringing her treats and making sure she was always comfortable; the team from the gallery, no doubt brightly dressed to the nines and, in sharp contrast, her singing friends in stark black.

I cannot think who else will be here. I phoned my brother four days ago but I have not heard from him since. He was in Florida. He and Crita were about to embark on their fifth cruise in a year. I doubt he will turn up and if he does he will know to come to the front and sit near me.

Who else? Her Newfoundland people … I hope not. I did make it clear to them at the hospital that I would rather they did not turn up here. It wouldn't be appropriate. They spent years rejecting me, not accepting that the two of us loved each other, so why be here today? Today is my day, she is not here anymore so their place is not here either. They did come to hospital and show that they cared for her then, or even try reconciliation with me. But now she is gone why this pretence? They never accepted her really. I never felt welcome in that large family. Her mother was always kind to me but out of her five brothers and sisters, none of them ever showed me any affection. When their mother died they kept Jo at a distance. Jo was good, too good for them. She forgave them all, their slight and spite. But I can't.

The music is starting. Members of her choir are standing at the back and singing *La Messe des Morts*. She used to play Andre Campras when rainy days kept us inside. It sometimes drove me mad, I found it too religious. But it is very beautiful. With my eyes closed, she is near, so near. The voices have reached a crescendo and then seem to die away.

Steps resonate in the room, I open my eyes: I can hardly believe it, three figures are making their way to the bench across the aisle. I clasp my hands together. I am shaking slightly. Henry must have noticed: as we sit down, he presses my elbow. Minutes pass, I try to contain my rage. They have appropriated that space as if she was theirs in equal measure. They cannot claim her now she has died. I won't give them the pleasure of looking at them.

Henry is standing by the coffin. It looks so small. She wasn't tall but I cannot believe that she is now contained in that wooden box and that soon there will be nothing left of her. Will my memories, a few photos and her poems be enough to keep her alive?

She would have been seventy-three in March, we could have had many years ahead of us still. Quiet, peaceful years; I want to cry for the walks, the films, the meals, the days and the nights, the conversations, the coming months and years we won't share. I want to weep for all those things that measure time and for the blank, empty canvas that the future has become.

Henry's few words are very touching. He wipes his eyes, I hear sniffling, bags being opened, rummaged through, I guess tears are being shed around me. I am determined to keep mine to myself. I control the welling inside me. I am quite good at doing that, have always been. My mother did not approve of tears or public outbursts of emotion. Another song. A solo this time. And then it is the end. Another one – the past few months have been filled with endings and I suppose this is the most significant of all.

I'm standing at the door. People are queuing up, they want to share with me the bits of their life with Jo, they want to say a good word about her, about us. I say a few things to each one, trying to respond in the way she would have. It is easier than I thought. Jo's brother and sister approach, they're with the third figure I saw earlier, a young woman, a niece maybe. I don't know her. She might be the girl Jo talked about, a student at McGill's I think. The other two have not really changed, put on some weight and greyed a bit. I look directly into their eyes, then turn around, take Henry's arm and walk away. Remote piano notes, familiar but too distant to identify, follow me to the car.

Now they have all gone. It has been a long day, at last I am on my own. It was good of them all to help me tidy up. The door is locked. The sofa. I will lie down for a while and will all thoughts to vanish ... Funny how I can still see these tiny lights through my eyelids. It is pretty, all sparkly. Yes, pretty...

✾

"Should I stay or should I go? Should I stay or should I go?" Annoying, that beat's been in my head all day, that's how Uncle Pete started the day at breakfast and I just can't shake it off... He's always been a sucker for English rock, even now aged sixty or so, he knows of obscure contemporary British bands. *The Clash*, he said. Never heard of them but the lyrics have suited today's mood. And now I'm standing there, outside Jo and Sarah's door, and wondering: should I stay or should I go? Sarah might be asleep. It's been a long day for her and she's probably not expecting anyone at this time.

Mum and Uncle Pete couldn't believe that she turned her back on us after the ceremony, but I don't really blame her. They haven't exactly had an open door policy with Jo since Grandma died. In fact, though mum never told me, I once found the photocopy of a letter addressed to both Jo and Sarah in which it was made pretty clear to them that nobody back home approved of their relationship. They've tried to mend things a bit since Jo's been ill but I guess it hasn't been enough to erase the past.

If I leave it any longer I will lose my nerve. I'm going for it.

The doorbell makes an interesting sound; sort of oriental. A succession of faint sounds from behind that door. She seems to pause after each step that brings her closer to me. I imagine her movements; careful, in slow motion. She looked young and fit earlier in the day but I think she's in her late seventies. Finally she opens the door, just enough to see me.
"Good evening," my voice quivers. "I'm Nina. I hope I'm not disturbing you."
"Well, actually you are. It has been a rather long day and I am tired."
She reaches for the handle and is about to close the door in my face. But then her eyes look straight into mine. I'm not sure what she sees there but she pauses and leaves it ajar.
"But I suppose that if you've come all the way here you would like to come in."
"Yes, but really I don't want to intrude."
"Don't worry, there is nobody here except for this old carcass of mine and the few trapped thoughts rattling around inside it."
She's cutting, crude and seems rather pleased with herself. Maybe it's

one of the good things that come with age.

The laces of my builders' boots are sodden and difficult to undo. Finally I step inside. The corridor opens onto a sitting room. I stand at the entrance, startled. It's stunning. I'm not quite sure what I'd expected; a dark interior, a musty smell, something in any case that would remind me of how old Jo was, of how old Sarah is, but not this. It seems that hundreds of fragile, flickering lights are illuminating the room, bouncing back off the white walls, bringing life to photographs that appear to be floating around the furniture. It must have taken Sarah ages to light all the candles. There are about thirty or forty of them, all white but of different sizes.

"Would you like something to drink? Tea, wine, something stronger?"

"I'll have whatever you're having."

Sarah disappears into the small kitchen. I look around. Neat rows of glasses on mirrored trays, washed and dried, empty bottles stacked up in boxes in a corner of the room. The photographs are mostly of trees, lone large trees or underwoods, branches and trunks, with smooth or rough bark, and intricate knots. Most of them are in black and white. A few photos portray people, either close-ups of their faces or their backs. Again and again a shape I recognise: Jo, I think. Whether trees or eyes, they all seem to capture a moment, a movement. The person behind the camera has caught an image and given it a new life on glossy paper.

Sarah returns with two crystal tumblers filled with amber liquid. More light, more warmth. None of this fits in with the picture of Jo and the "dirty fucking dyke" that my uncles used to laugh about when they referred to the woman Jo had brought home.

"Here, have a whisky." says Sarah. I'm not sure about whisky. I don't mind beer, I even enjoy a good Bierbrier but that's all. I don't think I have a choice though.

"Thank you. That will warm me up."

Sarah then lifts her glass and looking down, she says, "This one is for Jo."

The silence that falls between us sounds like a prayer.

The whisky makes its way down my throat, a burning sensation spreads itself. I feel I am glowing from inside, my flesh is melting into the room, becoming another flickering light.

Sarah sits down on the sofa and looks up.
"It's OK if you sit down. And really, I would like to know why you have come here tonight."

Of course in my head I've rehearsed an explanation but my words pour from me unexpectedly, and once out they feel like raindrops on a window. They've lost their shape, their meaning.
"I'm sorry to intrude, I wanted to speak to you. I would like to really get to know Jo – silly that it's posthumous. I knew of her but I never knew her, I remember meeting her as a little girl. She made quite an impression on me: she was always kind, funny, interested in the child I was. And she seemed so strong, calm, different from the other women I knew, so different from her sisters. I feel guilty: two years ago, I joined McGill, after High School you know. And I wanted to come and see you, but time went by, the way it does, and I procrastinated, got involved in student life, started seeing this guy. More time went by and then she became ill and by the time I got the courage to turn up at the hospital, she was really quite sick. I thought we could talk, that I could get to know her, but it was too late. And now, you're all that's left to bring me close to what she was. I'm sorry."
It's hard to keep the tears inside.

Sarah's quiet. Looking at her feet, which she's propped up on an old trunk. Then she turns to me and, pointing to the desk that almost rests against the back of the sofa, she asks, "Could you please get me the blue scrapbook? Over there on the desk?" She points to a thick book sitting in the middle of the desk. It's heavy and covered with soft, blue faded felt; unruly bits of paper stick out of it at odd angles. I pick it up.

As I hand it to her she rests her hand on it and in a low voice says, "You are right. You should be sorry. It is not well timed and you belong to that clan that hurt her so much, that ostracised her. Good thing it was that you lived so far away. But I suppose you are you, not them, and you are young. We all make mistakes. We don't always know how little time there is, how precious things are. I may not understand but, wherever she is, she will."
She takes the book from my hands and opens it.

"Ok should we start at the beginning?"

I nod and crane my neck to see the book now resting on her lap. She strokes the cover. Her movements slow, gentle. Her hands are very thin, but beautiful, her fingernails short, a perfect oval shape with a hint of clear varnish. Her thumb wipes away a tear that has fallen on the blue felt. I don't know what to say. There's nothing to say.

She opens the book and leafs through the pages. They're filled with verses, notes, doodling and collages, stuffed with scraps of paper and photographs. Then she goes back to the first page. There's a photograph of the two of them, Jo and Sarah, standing outside the Outremont town hall, brandishing an anti-Vietnam war banner.

"Mid sixties: we met. She had just started working at the St Sulpice Library as an English Literature librarian, and I was here for a six month assignment."

A few pages on, there's a poem written in purple ink, I can't make out the words. Opposite: a picture of my grandmother standing in front of a Volkswagen van, outside her house and, holding her arm, Sarah.

"1971. We were so in love that summer. We'd been going out for five or six years and in the spring we had moved in together. Around us people were getting married or having babies. Some seemed to be in stable relationships, some were still looking for Mr or Mrs Right and others were playing the field. We were the first ones out of our gay network who had decided to live together though. And proud of it. We had told my brother and he didn't seem too surprised. We needed to tell Jo's brothers and sisters. She had told her mother about us two years before but now she wanted me to meet her and the rest of the family. So that summer we decided to travel to Saskatchewan. We had a mixed welcome. Your grandmother was open, loving to me too and non-judgemental. But I was surprised by how unfriendly her five siblings were; they could barely hide their disapproval."

She turns the pages. Pictures of places, people, more purple writing as well as newspaper cuttings.

"Seventies, early eighties. Life was good. Jo went home regularly, every so often I flew back to New York. We did these trips on our own. They enabled us to reconnect with our old selves and the ghosts from the past without feeling any weight or sense of embarrassment. And then we'd come back, refreshed. Jo started writing poetry and with a few friends published *The Maple Leaf,* a bi-annual magazine. I immersed myself in my work as a photographer and with Henry, whom you probably saw in hospital as well as today, I started up a gallery. Your grandmother came for visits. We were happy, fulfilled and together."

A plane ticket and a church service sheet are stuck in very neatly on the next two pages. Photographs of my grandmother too. Sarah carries on: "1985. Your grandmother died and we both flew to Newfoundland. Jo's older sister – gosh I can't even remember her name – was staying in the family home: she'd had to travel from Toronto. She claimed that the house was full with all her kids. But there seemed to be no space for us in anybody's home so we ended up staying in a hotel. Jo was very sad. I was just angry'.

"I think I remember," I interrupt her. "I was just a little girl but there is a picture in my mind of Jo, standing outside our front door, and crying. Years later, when I was sixteen, I stood outside that same door, which I'd slammed shut, and I cried too. My parents didn't know I was there. They didn't open the door to try and see where I'd gone. I was there for a long time and the image of Jo, which I'd buried somewhere in the folds of my memory, came back vividly. In it she was wearing a long violet scarf. Six months later I'd left home."

Sarah's hand now presses mine and she says: "She did have a violet scarf." Then she takes her hand away and sighs heavily, more like she's trying to catch her breath. The moment passes and we go back to the book.

The following pages contain photographs of small things and more writing but, I notice, no more verse.

"Life went on. Twenty years or so, I guess. Typically, she forgave them. Went back for your uncle Jerry's funeral and even your cousin Sally's wedding. *The Maple Leaf* did not survive the eighties. She stopped writing poetry. Something had been broken. A belief she had maybe. She started singing. If she couldn't find within herself the words to express beauty and love and life, she could be the voice that would carry the words others had found. She belonged to a choir. They specialised in sacred music. Her voice was always young, beautiful. We discovered she had cancer because she was finding it increasingly difficult to sing higher

notes. We had her throat examined and that's when they told us."
She turns to me and looks into my eyes.
"And I suppose you know the rest."
More words are said, about the past, the present too. I quiz her on her photographs and she asks what I do at McGill. Seems genuinely interested. We have another whisky.

It's now getting late. I should be going, I've found out a lot, about Jo, and about my family. Myself too. It's all so sad. So much unhappiness has been caused. As I'm lacing up my boots, I blurt out, "How about meeting up tomorrow? For coffee? Or something?"
I don't quite know why I suggested it. Maybe I want to put things right. Maybe I just want to spend an afternoon with her. She's bitter when it comes to us all but she's also fascinating.
"Why not? I don't think I have anything on."
"Do you know the Café des Arts down in the French quarter?"
"You mean in the Bonsecours Gallery?"
"Yes, there's an exhibition down there right now. Some artist by the name of Fung Sou. Vietnamese, a woman. You'll like it, I think."
"It sounds good, let's hook up tomorrow then, around three."
She doesn't move towards me but watches me go down the steps and then I hear her shut the door.

✄

I look out of the window. I've been looking out all morning. I am now used to Jo not being around first thing. To getting up as soon as I wake up, to breakfasts on my own. But my mornings, my days were spent in hospital, watching the time go by, irreversibly. Making the most of every little thing to spruce up her life. Today, for the first time in a long while, I'm looking out at the outside world. It's a blue, bright and freezing day, there are icicles hanging from the window frame, but it's blurred by her absence. I'm still alive but I feel dead really. She was my means and my end, flesh and blood. Tomorrow. There will be a tomorrow and another. And I will have to carry on, to find the strength from somewhere within me and from the people and things around me.

It's time to go. I'm not quite sure why I agreed to meeting Nina, I would much rather stay here. But she didn't give me her telephone number; I can't cancel. She was nice. Nicer than I thought she would be. Her eyes were so like Jo's. And her hair too. It was the strand of red hair coming out of her funny black hat that made me open the door.

I want to walk to *Marche Bonsecours* in Old Montreal. If I go now I can stop a few times on the way and be there for three. That walk used to take me 45 minutes, now it's more like an hour and a half. Time does that to you. Ironic really, the less time you have ahead of you, the more time it takes to do everything. Wrapped in a long red puffer jacket I take the wooden stick I was given years ago when I used to hike. And for some reason I put the scrapbook in my large satchel. Nina might want to have another look.

It is as cold as I had imagined. My breath forms little clouds that float ahead of me. On the ground the new blank canvas that formed overnight is already marked by a thousand imprints. The snow is still crisp though, every footstep makes a slight crackling noise. I like that. I dig my heel in first, then the rest of the foot. At first the snow caves in a bit. But somehow its icy resistance gives the heel enough momentum to make the next step. It's cold. My gloved hands are tucked into my pockets but my face is exposed to the bite of the air. It's not unpleasant. I slow down and try to concentrate on the things around me. First the trees, then the park as I leave Outremont; I picture Jo, looking ahead of her, on the bench under that old maple tree. Now its leaves are rotting on the ground. The same fate awaits us. Is all we have done and stood for that meaningless?

In spite of my fur-lined boots my feet feel frozen. I turn a corner and find myself surrounded by low houses and apartment blocks. There are kids playing outside; I try to imagine the grown ups around here, their concerns, food, washing, the little ones to look out for, dress and keep warm. Their lives so very different from ours. I think of the picture of her with her siblings, the one she kept in her wallet when we first met. The six of them sitting on a wall, bruised knees and large smiles, squinting at the camera. She loved them so much and I think they loved her too, in their own way. Why could they not understand her better? She tried to reach out to them, to get through to them but it did not work. I suppose they never left home, never felt the need for it; I suppose they were caught up in their lives, their kids, the food, the washing. Not enough time maybe to stop and think and decide to accept her difference.

The air seems less clear but the cold still bites, here at the heart of the city. It's bustling with people going about their business, which they probably see as being of global importance. How mighty do they think they really are, here, in New York, London, Hong Kong and all those money-making places? A dark suited man is coming towards me. He's probably just popped out of the office for a rubbery sandwich. Where the pavement narrows, he steps down, smiling, his eyes are blue. I walk on. That smile is within me, I cannot shake it off; my heart tightens and blood rushes to my head, filling me with heat; someone lovely was there underneath the suit. Is there always something lovely to find in everyone? Is there? I guess so.

I'm not sure whether the air is warmer in this part of town or whether it's because I have been walking for more than an hour, but I feel less cold. *The Vieux-Montreal*, as the "French" call it, is ahead of me: a world of its own, with its old streets and buildings. The Place Jacques Cartier looks rather beautiful today. I did say to Nina last night something about us all making mistakes. We do, we do. Jo was so good at forgiving.

I'd forgotten the uneven pebbled streets of Old Montreal. These last steps are difficult; my satchel feels heavy now. I'm tired but I am early. There is a gallery that sells some extraordinary objets d'art. Before Jo became ill, we would sometimes wander in and enjoy looking around. It is a bright room with views over the St Laurent and large glass panels that seem to glide open. There are all kinds of pottery and lamps; bright and of various and interesting forms. And today, in one corner of the room, there is a giant xylophone, the size of a piano. It is constructed on a wooden frame in the shape of a boat. The colours of the rainbow seem to have come together in this instrument: the bars are made of transparent glass and each is of a different colour and a different size. It's just beautiful. My hands move towards it. The bars are soft and cold, the wood is warmer. I pick up the two light mallets and gently let them glide over it. The sound that comes out is clear and pure and each bar gives out a very different note. Was this what God saw when he made the world and its people? How disappointing it must be, all this grief and sadness. It would be like looking at thousands of those glass bars, now shards, on the floor, mixed with bits of wood. Such chaos in hatred, I guess there is beauty in forgiveness.

I walk away. Nina will be here soon. I'm looking forward to seeing her now. I prop my stick against a table, put my bag on the back of the chair, take off my coat and sit down. The café is not too busy. The satchel is hanging behind me. I turn to see the bulge of the scrapbook. The book looks heavy but I know how light it is now. I wonder if Nina might like to have it.

March | Jamaica
Rachel Jackson

It was always this that she remembered, long after everything else had faded. This brick-hard hit of clinging, syrupy heat; a brutal and immediate assault of temperature on her face and lungs, followed by a softening, a relaxing, as if to say 'soon come'. This was the start of it, not the passport queue, or the holding of breath, albeit innocently, past the Customs' desk. It was only the scalding air that flung itself against her face and hair and rushed thickly into her nostrils as she paused to meet it at the top of the exit steps of the plane, which signalled that Dionne had arrived at the place her parents called Home: Jamaica.

The sharp corner of someone's hand-luggage pushed at her back, reminding her to move forward, which she did, uncertainly. Her black heels, the footwear in which she preferred to greet her destinations – most recently Madrid and New York – helped to slow her steps. What they gave in stature and sense of occasion they took away in comfort and stability as she descended to the tarmac.

Dionne breathed in the molasses-rich air and picked up the pace, all the sooner to enter the airport building. Inside, travellers snaked through the formalities, brandishing passports, soothing infants, clicking mobile phones back to life. She took her place up by the luggage carousel, left hand holding open *The Daily Telegraph*, right hip thrust out to keep her steady. There it was, at the bottom of page three: Thousands of Couples Lose Out In IVF Lottery. She didn't bother to read it, not yet. Give it a few months, she might want nothing more than to be poring over every pitying word, making notes, calling helplines. But she did not wish to be part of that stricken, pleading world any sooner than she had to. If she could just get through the next fortnight and straight back home, they would still have one good night this month.

As she straightened, the noise hit her. This fruity babble of families discussing meeting relations, catching connections, checking out hotel pools. The sounds of Norman Manley International flooded her ears, bursts of sense throwing themselves up from the insistent, deafening murmur:

"I think it this way. Hurry child."

"Mummy, can Tilly and I share a room?"

"Ten days an' she never ask me once."

"Taxi? Anyone wan' taxi?"

The excitement fizzed around her without truly sinking under her skin. Right now Mike would be sitting at his desk, firing off snappy, typo-strewn e-mails or writing a report that would keep him at his desk until dinner time. She'd left a first night lasagne, to make things easier, although he would probably find it easier still to stay out at the watering hole around the corner from the office.

With a small jolt she spotted her scarlet suitcase approaching. Hauling it off with a backwards totter, she turned and walked the Customs route. She waded through the noise to the exit, the arrivals' catwalk, only to be impaled upon a sharp screech of excitement.

"She here! Look, she here!"

Dionne clocked the large, bouncy woman, waving a name sign with two plump hands. She responded in the only way that seemed appropriate, with a delighted smile.

Her cousin, perhaps? And what about the young boy next to her? Now six or seven people were grinning in her direction and bobbing excitedly, not one face among them that she recognised. She strode towards them, over-smiling, her face displaying the confidence she did not feel.

"Hello," she said, too brightly. "I'm Dionne."

"We know that, girl," cried the sign woman. "Come here!"

Without waiting for Dionne to get past the barrier, the woman leant over the metal railing and gave her an extraordinary hug, both firm and squashy, absorbing her in a rich fug of cocoa butter.

"You not know me now? Ah, I'm Beryl," she leant back and waved around at the surrounding faces. "Agnes, Miss Gaynor, Sonny, Leroy, Anthony, Darling. You'll meet the rest back home."

"Pleased to meet you," she offered, still smiling, trying to piece together the picture. Beryl she now recalled, a cousin through Auntie Pat. The unforgettably-named Darling was a cousin too, a heavily pregnant younger cousin, though from which aunt or uncle she was not too sure. Miss Gaynor was no blood relative, but a close friend of her mother's, like a sister to her, or had been once... Before she could jam any more pieces into place she was being waved around the barrier and swept towards the exit. After a few yards they were at the cars, and she was ushered into a faded red saloon, along with Beryl, Sonny and either Anthony or Leroy. The others piled into a rusty truck parked behind and then they were off.

As soon as the airport was behind them, with much tooting and waving at people she had assumed were strangers, Beryl was off too, cheerfully, deafeningly, on a seemingly endless explanation.
"You see, Darling was gonna come wit' her new man but he baby sick, but all good 'cos Miss Gaynor so please to come too, an' she know you before you born. It's Sonny say Darlin' too big wi' her own baby soon come, but him jus' being foolish. Him think he know everything there is. Not England though, never been nowhere. Anthony say to Sonny, he gonna go to England some day an' Agnes say you is living somewhere real nice, London, though she only seen it on Benjamin's television. It's like I say, nothing see, nothing know..."
Dionne clung on to the handle of the passenger door, listening to the seamless patter of Beryl, who unfortunately was driving and not letting that small fact distract her from her main business of telling her guest just how things were. They jolted and weaved through the potholes of Kingston then further out and on, past glossy stumps of banana trees, onto barely passable tracks, through fields of shimmering sugar cane, out west, on and on towards the beaches of Negril.

Four hours of chatter were still ringing in her ears as she showered in the small bathroom at Beryl's house. The size of the place had surprised her – bigger than she remembered from childhood, when it was surely supposed to be far smaller. Perhaps her nine-year old eyes had once baulked at the thought of three generations living in one wood and brick farm, having last cast their gaze upon her own generous, redbrick, Hertfordshire home. Or perhaps she now knew that this much space and comfort, though modest, was more than enough when the sun licked your back every day and mangoes dropped from the trees in your own fenceless acres. In her youth she had thought of her Negril cousins as dirt poor; now every early-retiring stockbroker and his wife would kill for a lush piece of real estate like this. Not to mention the Caribbean approach to the work-life balance. She scrunched her eyes tighter under the stream of water, wondering at the prim little English miss she must have seemed.

As she reached for the towel that she'd nearly forgotten to pack, there was Agnes's unembarrassed head through the door, teeth gleaming white save for the one proud gold cap.
"We gon eat soon. Y'alright?"
Dionne, pulled the towel to her so that it hung awkwardly over her breasts and stomach.
"I'm fine thanks. Out in a minute."
Agnes smiled wider and withdrew, leaving the door ajar. Dionne rolled her eyes and started to rub herself dry. Why had she imagined that she would feel instantly at home here, that she could fill her mother's flat, wide-fit shoes in Negril? Jamaican by blood she might be, but so what? What did any of that mean when that blood had been chilled by thirty-four years of English winters and stirred by loving a white man from Hull and heated by the passions and politics and prejudices of another country altogether? Two weeks had made sense back in London, what with the lengthy flight times and all. Naked in Negril they now seemed like two weeks to be spent as a known stranger; two weeks filled with misunderstandings and fake smiles and a feeling that she really should be at home, ovulating and ready in her Agent Provocateur.

She pulled on her favourite sunshine yellow day dress and hurried back into the bedroom. Kicking on flip-flops she went through to the kitchen where she found all the women – Beryl, Agnes, Darling and Miss Gaynor – frying plantain, kneading johnny cakes, stirring sticky rice and tossing herbs into a pungent stew. A few young children ran in from outside and were quickly waved away again. The men were nowhere and didn't seem missed.

"Can I do something?" she offered.

"You can tek grandmom this." Beryl held a glass of yellow juice out to her. "Thank you."

Dionne took the glass and turned away, not knowing where to go next. Grandmom, right. She tried the door opposite and found a tiny empty bedroom. Another door further to the right yielded Sonny lying on his bed. Every door was knocked on and tried, but none opened to reveal an aged grandmother. She moved to the back door and looked across the yard. There were a few other buildings and sheds, the only one of which was worth approaching was a small white and turquoise bungalow. Stepping through the dirt she saw that the door was ajar and crept inside, taking care not to slop the juice.

The familiar old woman sat ramrod straight in the only chair in the room, watching a small television propped up on a dresser. Not yet realising she was being observed she seemed imperious, as if waiting for the TV to dare to offend her. Then she turned her head and her face creased into a modest smile.

"You Dionne?"

"Yes Grandma, that's me."

"Welcome, you grown big." She turned back to the television, where a couple were dancing in lurid pink clothes. "You come for my birthday?"

"Yes, I have," she replied. "From England."

"You're a good girl." She did not move her eyes from the screen and seemed to have closed the subject. Dionne crept forward and put the juice down on a small table. She started to back quietly out of the room, as if in the presence of royalty, then realised what she was doing and turned properly to go, feeling annoyance rise. Almost five thousand miles and the only relative she remembered, the one whose eightieth birthday party invitation had called for her to come, would rather watch TV. Suddenly the irritation burst out into a small laugh. Right now she could be with her husband, making things happen, not like they had all the time in the world, after all. But she shouldn't bitch – it was hot, it was Jamaica, goddamn paradise, so they said. She would simply go inside and try to swallow something down about these people she had long forgotten, along with some mouthfuls of curried goat.

Back in the kitchen, Sonny, Leroy and Anthony were mixed in with the women, along with two older men she didn't recognise. No one introduced her so she said nothing to them. The table, covered in a lacy cloth, was laid out with a vast bowl of spicy stew, another huge tub of rice, a platter of hot dumplings and some fried plantain. At some unseen signal the children dashed in from outside, trailing dust. Everyone moved to a chair or stool, or for the youngest, a spot on the floor.

Dionne sunk into a chair just as Grandmom entered, leaning on her stick, and giving an impatient flick of her free hand that made Leroy leap to help with her chair.
Beryl, still standing, held up her hand and spoke.
"Lord, for this lovely food on our table, may we be truly grateful. Amen. You can start now."
Hands got busy spooning stew and crispy dumplings, jaws started to eagerly chat and chew whilst Dionne hesitated, not wanting to lean halfway across the table for food.
"What wrong girl?" Beryl shouted at her from the head of the table. "You not hungry?"
"No, I'm... definitely," she stammered, reaching across her neighbour for the rice.
Suddenly there was loud and urgent buzzing. Her Blackberry, left out on the sideboard, was vibrating hard against the wood. Maybe Mike had finally picked up her message. Judging the mood to be sufficiently buoyant and chaotic, she shoved her chair back and reached behind her to take a quick look at the text.

Hey babe. Glad your flight ok. Bet it's not as hot there as you. Speak later. P.S. Don't have a rum punch for me!
A surge of affection washed over the slight nip of irritation she felt at being reminded not to drink, and rinsed it away.
She left the phone on the side and scraped back closer to the food. Next to her was Darling, face half-hidden by an elaborate cloud of braids and curls, assiduously piling her plate high. Dionne did the same, her appetite suddenly blooming.
"Darling, have you been to England?"
"No never been. You got man in England?"

"Yes, Mike. He wanted to come but, you know... work."

"Right. Children?"

"No. Not yet."

"This my second baby. Three month more to wait."

"Congratulations," she started forking her food. Darling couldn't be much over twenty.

"That depend," said Darling. She speared a piece of goat and looked away.

It made sense that she would spend her first full day at Bloody Bay Beach. It was the place she could remember most clearly from her childhood trips to Negril and when Leroy had shyly asked if she wanted to go anywhere it was the only place she could think of. She followed him outside clutching a towel and bag of beach necessities, flushing slightly as she walked past Beryl who was sweeping out the kitchen like a woman with only one mission in life. Leroy walked towards the family car, then straight past it turning onto a narrow, beaten down path in the garden. They trampled on at an unreasonable pace through glossy green bushes and past pink bougainvillea for several minutes, without Leroy once turning back to speak to her. Dionne was starting to get uncomfortable, flip-flopping hard in the sun, dodging imagined spiders and grass snakes, wondering about the wordless Leroy and trying to figure out how they were related, if at all. She was trying to summon the breath to ask him about their family when he turned sharply left and started jogging down a slope. She trotted behind him until she saw it too, the same expanse of gleaming sand and impossibly clear sea where she had tasted her first sky juice and shelled her first guinep.

She breathed her thanks to Leroy who just nodded and pointed at a spot just ahead of them, presumably where she might lie. As she walked over to it he did not follow, trudging instead further up the beach towards a middle-aged Rasta in yellow trunks who was sitting fifty yards away whittling at something. The only other person on the beach.

Dionne experienced a rising thrill at having been left alone. She laid out her towel, smoothing it down, pulling out the sun cream and bottled water with no one to see her and notice that, black as she was, she too was simply an overcautious tourist. Sitting on the towel, arms pulling up her knees, she stared out into the endless turquoise of the Caribbean. Her eyes glazed and blurred, sweat beading on her brow as she gazed into the bright sea, thinking of nothing except how, if you tried hard enough, it was entirely possible to be perfectly absent, to be completely elsewhere in the world. She could not remember the last time she felt so alone and in the stunning heat and brightness, it was easy to confuse it with freedom.

The buzz made her kick out a foot in surprise, spraying her towel with a smattering of sand. She really had to turn this thing off. She picked up the Blackberry and there he was, Mike. The button was clicked impatiently. *Hi hon. How's the 'family'? McGlenn deal came in thank god, loads more work. Miss you. You on the beach yet?*
She put down the phone and tried to re-engage with the view, irritation pulsing in her stomach. She picked up the phone and read it again. There it was, the weird punctuation, the 'family'. That single, smug little nod to her perfectly summed up what she had suspected since he had told her he wouldn't be able to make the trip, eightieth birthday or not. Her family, with its steps and halves and mysterious links and marriage-less connections was not quite real to him. Not a bit like his solid, two-child, still-married parent family from the sturdy, hard-working north. Nor indeed like the family they themselves could be, with a sizeable mortgage, enviable prospects and a plump newborn. No, her family, rarely thought of, much less understood, needed to be put in speech marks.

She scrambled up and walked quickly over the throbbing sand to the water's edge. When she eased her feet into the sea it was as if she could taste salt at the back of her throat. A glance to her left took in Leroy and the Rasta, talking like brothers, one still whittling, the other nodding hard and laughing. Their easiness together calmed her down, although she was not part of it. It settled her mind enough to let in the thoughts she had decided not to entertain until some other time, later, back home.

What if there never was a baby? What if the booze-free months of careful eating and diligently tarted-up lovemaking produced nothing at all save a sense of loss that started out smarting like a pulled tooth and ended up aching like a missing limb? The confidence they had tacitly, mutually agreed to project might only survive a few hard disappointments and perhaps after a fifth of sixth failure, it would crumple like a battered bedsheet.

The thought drew her forward, pulling her deeper into the cool water, up to her knees, then her thighs. She scooped up two palmfuls of water in cupped hands, lifted them high and let them pour onto her burning face. Success was the cleanser, the only thing that would do.

Reaching their goal would be the most fragrant way in which to wipe over the memories that still nagged and bit at her as she tried to sleep most nights. A baby, with its demands and mesmerising stare and never-ending cries for love, would surely wipe her mind clean of the times when, less certain of their intentions perhaps, they had both been tempted to explore other options. The water was now lapping at her breasts. She drew a large breath and ducked under.

Bursting back through the surface, she turned to look back at the beach. The men were still seated. She could not tell if they were watching her, but preferred to think they were not. There were times when a girl needed to be alone, just to prove she could be. She had proven a lot to herself recently, not least that she possessed an excellent ability to pretend to forget. But what would all that forgetting and burying down and blanking out ultimately be without their jointly-made new life, their success? The thought felt uncomfortably close to disloyalty. She would, after all, still have Michael. But the Michael she would have was a man who had never willingly looked unfulfilled desire in the eye: he got what he wanted. She would have Michael, but he would not have his 'family'.

Eight candles, one for every decade. The cake looked like it was made of chocolate and coconut, a confection with an air of puffed up pride about it, a centrepiece. Beryl, of course, was the one to bring it to the table, clucking gently at the smiles of approval. Grandmom sat as straight as she could, unsmiling, as if it was her unquestionable duty to bring dignity to the ritual.

There had to be sixty people, some in the room, some out, others darting here and there, particularly the teenagers who dived into the ackee and saltfish like hungry magpies then flitted off again to flirt and whisper by the outhouses. Dionne waited for someone to start up Happy Birthday, which eventually came, long after the cake, from a man in a porkpie hat who looked older than Grandmom herself. Everyone, save the vanished teens, joined in, in a rich, surprisingly harmonious chorus. Grandmom nodded and permitted herself her first smile of the evening, a benevolent crescent that showed no teeth. Soon after, Sonny was beckoned to escort her to bed and the jumping soca was turned up louder; the teenagers sloped back.

The men pushed the table back against the wall and Darling was soon upon her, grabbing Dionne's hands and shaking her hips in an impressive manner for one so pregnant. Dionne laughed and shook her own hips harder, determined not to be outdone. She may have spent the past five days on Bloody Bay Beach and browsing the markets like a stranger, an American even, with only dollars and good manners as currency, but this was her music too. More than that, she now knew, from small confidences shared over a ripe mango on the kitchen steps or a cold, illicit Red Stripe in the yard, things that she could take back home with her, things that mattered. Like the fact Leroy was no blood relation at all but was still to be considered family, having fathered a child to a cousin who later took off with some Kingston boy. His child was one of those that ran up and down the porch step each day, a burstingly plump and pretty girl of about four. She could also take home the fact that Darling was very much in love with her boyfriend, but the boyfriend was not too in love with the idea of becoming daddy again and was spending too much time in Montego Bay. That would sit next to the fact that Grandmom had given birth to nine children, the surviving five of whom had formed the roots of her Jamaican family. Things she had not known before, things that Mike had never asked, things that took the speech marks away from her family. She shook her hips hard and when Sonny, elated, shouted "Jump, jump!" she jumped.

They were plucking chickens. It was a surreal sight, one that seemed as if it might have been specially laid on as a spectacle to shock the 'hinglish' girl. But no, there they were, Beryl and Darling, determinedly pulling the feathers out of two dead birds, with a third lying, neck broken, on the kitchen table. Dionne hesitated in the doorway: to enter would surely be mistaken for a sign of readiness to pluck, which at eight thirty or so in the morning, it was most decidedly not. Before she could say 'coffee, please' the matter was settled for her.

"You up now?" smiled Beryl. "Come, sit, take the hen."

Dionne smiled wanly and took her place at the table, too dismayed to even feel nausea as she picked up the lifeless bird. She had done this before, sort of, once, but it had been part of a stoned week in Cornwall with some smallholding friends. Then it had been absolutely in the spirit of things, now it just felt like a very bad alternative to breakfast. Beryl was chatting, very fast, to Darling, in proper patois now, not the carefully enunciated version of Jamaican she had used when Dionne first arrived. Flattering really, it meant that they were used to her being around; she was nothing special, like them, family. Even so, she could barely make out what was being said, so she simply tugged hard at the chicken's back feathers and tried not to tear the skin.

Just as a small bald patch was starting to appear, the two other women rose, brushing feathers from their laps and slung their finished chickens into a pot. Still garbling at each other, they ambled to the front door and went off outside without another word to Dionne.

It was harder still to pluck the bird without an audience. The warm body with its clouded eyes seemed to reproach her for prolonging its humiliation, although, even without the benefit of caffeine, she knew this to be absurd. She was just contemplating the best way to speed up the process, when a large stone seemed to hit the front door. She turned and instead saw a walking stick bashing the door open. Grandmom.

"Dionne?" the old woman murmured as she leaned into the room, as if surprised to see her.

"Yes grandmom, good morning."

"What you doin' to dat hen, leave it be, Darling can do it."

She sounded almost angry and Dionne let the bird fall onto the table, feeling foolish.

Grandmom held out the cane and used it to hook a chair leg, pulling the seat back towards her. Then, very slowly, she lowered herself to the table next to her guest.

"You mus' be look forward to going back to England, my right?"

Dionne smiled brightly "Not really, all that cold... It's beautiful here."

Her smile was met with a shake of the head.

"But you got man. You not miss him already?"

"Yes, of course," she replied, maintaining the smile.

"He angry you here?"

"No!" she exclaimed, glancing at the humiliated chicken. "No, it's different back in London. Busy, you know, we both have to do our own thing..."

"Don't sound so good to me."

Dionne let the smile fade, defeated. Grandmom was sitting back straight as ever, her mouth moving like she was chewing gum. Dionne waited.

"Ting is," she eventually pronounced, looking down at the floor as if the feathers displeased her. "Ting is, if a man let you come here alone, mus' be you or he not happy."

Dionne let her gaze fall to the feathers, a protest ready on her lips that could not quite make its way out. She stared at the white down covering the floor, groping for a lie which evaded her. She tilted her chin up again.

"We're not, actually. He wants a baby and I'm not pregnant so... So."

Grandmom was still chewing, staring down some invisible flaw on the far wall of the kitchen. Dionne could hear the rapid murmur of Beryl somewhere in the backyard. Some moments later Grandmom spoke again.

"He want baby or he want you?"

"I don't know," she replied immediately. "That's the problem I just don't know."

At that point the old woman chose to look her in the eye.

"You sound all wound up tight. Seem to me your man don't know neither, my right?"

"Probably," Dionne could feel herself deflating slowly.

Grandmom poked her stick into the feather on the floor, clearing them from around her chair.

"Then seem to me baby got no business wit' you two."

She dug her cane hard into the floor and slowly rose to leave, all chewing ceased.

"Beryl be pleased," she added when fully upright. "Too many babies round here anyhow."

Just like that. As if Islington were just a suburb of Kingston and any child of Dionne's would naturally be skidding in and out of this very kitchen, stealing tamarind balls and getting under everyone's feet. As if she lived there. Grandmom slowly made her way out of the kitchen, happy to leave Dionne alone with the abused bird. As she reached the top step she called back without turning.

"May as well do that chicken. Darling busy sweeping the yard."

Just like that. As if she lived there.

Hi babe. Really sorry but don't think can collect you from airport. Need to go to London, explain later. Call me when free. X

She seriously thought about phoning, as she looked up at the glistening rows of green sugar cane and settled back against the rock, the cold beer bottle held loosely in her hand. But four more days of Jamaica was all she had left. The little bits of communication she had had with Mike kept pulling her back to somewhere she wasn't ready to be: they felt intrusive, even when she was the one who called. He would have to wait, as would the talk that she had been rehearsing since the morning after Grandmom's party.

They had got the wrong idea. The baby, all wrong. She had always known it, which is perhaps why when she counted her most fertile days, fussed and plotted, abstained and arranged, she had been haunted by the feeling of playing a role and suppressing stage fright. Mike knew it too, which is perhaps why the McGlenn deal had taken on its mythical importance and perhaps why, despite everything, he was not with her for the most precious days this month.

The realisation seeped through her like a rising tide of relief. She lay back under the cane canopy, eyes closed, breathing in the good smells of dirt and the sweat from her walk. She was already nostalgic about the idea they had cooked up, now toying with the luxury of feeling amused and a little shocked. It seemed sweetly naive, almost innocent, but that time had passed, somewhere between Heathrow and the crooked roads of Negril. A baby was not a cleanser. She was not sure what it was, but it had never truly seemed to belong to her and Mike, even unborn, unconceived. Even little Darling would have seen that. She now needed to understand just what did belong to them, now that it had all changed. Bathing in the sickly sucrose smell of raw cane blown by a light breeze, she finally saw that change. The family that now spoke to her was not one waiting to be created, it was one asking to be discovered.

It was the second text message she had left unanswered. Eyes still shut, she groped for her phone, face upturned to an eager sun. Dionne looked at it and dialled the number reserved in her phone. Not Michael, the airline. If she could change her flight, just another week, another fortnight even, the right words might eventually come to her. The phone rang on and on but, under those sweet leaves, she was happy to wait.

April | New York
Alexa Hughes Wilson

Lizzie was lying on her side looking at Jonathan with one eye, the other eye was crushed down in the pillow she was hugging to her face and chest. It smelled like him, like their old life.

"Johnny, awake?"

"No. I'm staring at the ceiling in my sleep. Sleep staring is a serious illness that affects untold thousands leading to dry eyes and in the extreme torn retinas."

Lizzie propped herself up on one elbow and drew the covers to her chin.

"Johnny, you know when you wake up... ."

She watched him slowly close his eyes like a cat.

"I'm not awake."

For a moment Lizzie paused, considering the little flickers of muscles in his eyelids.

"Then just sleep-listen."

"OK."

She rolled onto her back and considered the torn paper lantern hanging over the futon.

"You know when you first wake up in a familiar place, a place you've woken up so many times, but you can't figure out quite why you are there or when or even which you is waking up?"

Her attention shifted back to Jonathan, still pretending to sleep but with a faint smile teasing at the corners of his mouth.

"Your skin goes all tingly and your insides freeze... I panic. Late for an exam is always my first thought; late for teaching; late night gone wrong." Lizzie exhaled slowly. "Then it all begins to fall in place. The blood starts to circulate again and each memory and recognition wraps around you until you are fully... I don't know... modernised, the most up to date self available where those few moments earlier you were swimming around in all those other mornings and selves. It always happens when I go home to see my parents."

Jonathan half opened his eyes to look at her.

"That's pitiful."

"I know. Waking moment one: I am thirteen and I have not prepared for a math exam."

She rolled over and rested her head and hand on his shoulder. Across the horizon line of his chest, she studied the clouds chasing past the dirty window.

"Yup, but this morning it was really nice because I got a chance to be that crazy, sad Lizzie who lived here, dragged home strangers, wept on your shoulder, and was late to give exams... and then got my shit together and finished a degree and got engaged to a non-alcoholic (makes Paul sound like a beverage, oh well), non passive-aggressive, non aggressive-aggressive, intelligent, totally hot academic who even likes my cats... All that in one fuzzy moment. I feel rather accomplished already today."

Here her eyes finally met his. He tumbled her off his shoulder, sat up, shuffled for a cigarette in the pile of clothes next to him, started to light it, then paused.

"Lizzie, you know I don't actually like Paul."

Jonathan gave her a perplexed half-smile and turned back to light his smoke. After a few thoughtful drags, he drew his knees up to his chest.

"I dislike him because you act like your pants are too tight when you're around him. Nervous. Itchy even."

He stamped out the smoke and fixed her with what was the closest he had to a disapproving expression.

"With Paul, you always go home before the after-hours salsa clubs even get going and way before your 4am-sixty-year-old Puerto Rican lovers try to take you home."

"That man was so not trying to take me home last night; he was just a really good dancer."

"Yeah. And I have no problem with that. And you were having a ball. And if Paul had been with us? You would not have been experiencing the aerial side of tango while drinking shots of Tequila. I worry about that... I worry about you."

"Yeah. So would he. Look, I know that's not what you mean. Paul just doesn't think it's so much fun to see me flying around the city like a maniac even if he knows he's taking me home."

"Yeah. And I love seeing that. It is an art form few could imitate. Doesn't matter."

Jonathan's eyes were again glued to the ceiling of this ugly little room with its mishmash of angles, narrow metal window, and bad paint job. His eyes began roaming around the ceiling examining cracks and pocks. "I'm glad to have this apartment to myself so this room can be like it was when you lived here: the nothing room. The room is just like the view, bricks with sky, so it all boils down to the light."

A chilly, wan April light was falling all over the bricks on the opposite wall, barely making a mark inside the window.

"Stop staring at the ceiling," Lizzie said it in a mock-gruff gravelly voice.

"Lizzie, you're naked."

"I know, so are you... whatever, it's the nothing room as originally intended."

And with joking fanfare, she tossed off the covers.

Jonathan sucked in his breath and then sighed.

"Lizzie, I still want to hop on you. Even after two years of practising not wanting to... I haven't quite gotten the knack yet. I know its lovely we've always been able to sleep together without necessarily sleeping together, but it was so much nicer when the possibility was there."

"And I suppose that has nothing to do with your lack of enthusiasm about Paul?"

She squeezed her lips up into a silly pout and crossed her eyes.

Without shifting his upward gaze, Jonathan felt around for the pack of smokes and lighter. Lizzie reached across him for the ashtray and placed it on his chest.

"Thanks. I would call it objection 7 a. ii, which just gives you an idea of how complex and myriad my objections are. And I am actually enjoying the ceiling probably more than I would enjoy gazing at your body draped over the sheets you left here when you moved. But best of all would be a really nice shower which we both know to be impossible in this apartment, so I'll just go cower under the Petrarchan nozzle. I burn; I freeze; I wash."

Nights out with Jonathan often ended like this... in the morning. They had so many old habits from the years they'd shared this place on East 11th St. Actually, it had just been two years, but so much seemed to happen to them all the time. He and Lizzie fell in love with great frequency and out of love, with each other, with other people and often all at the same time. They had never been really together in the way most couples are, but everyone else stayed on the outside of the intrigues. Both of them were slightly broken-hearted when they had moved in together and they had known each other for years already, back in Texas, so they knew the same people, songs, jokes, parties. Often newly minted lovers felt uncomfortable with the obvious intimacy between them, but they created this circus of dancing and laughing which could be inviting, especially after a good night out.

When Lizzie met Paul, Jonathan had been dating a gorgeous mad biologist for a while so her frequent nights away from East 11th had not made much of an impression on Jonathan. As a matter of fact, three months had passed without their usual cabal of late night stories, wanders, and sleeping together. Consequently when Johnny's biologist broke his heart, he was shocked to find his best friend and solace curled up on the other side of a duvet explaining that she had truly, properly, the way-she'd-sworn-she-never-would-again, fallen in love and was moving out, and in with Paul.

By the time Jonathan was out of the shower, Lizzie was back in her evening attire and heels, because she never planned to stay over, even when Paul was away as he had been last night. For the last two days, he had been up in Cambridge, MA delivering a paper for a neuropsychology conference. Soon he would be on a train heading home and in about eight hours they would be going to a colleague's Washington Square apartment for dinner. Actually it would be a dinner party, and of the kind that made you feel you had been awarded an honorary degree in something. Fascinating books tumbled off shelves onto tables; there was always someone from Bulgaria or Latvia who taught everyone a traditional toast poured out with some semi-toxic ancestral potion. You felt somewhat drunk and burnished walking down the steps at 2am, too drunk to be really clever anymore, but as if your aptitude for knowing what mattered in the world had just grown twofold. In about eight hours, about eight blocks west.

Jonathan was standing in the kitchen doorway, naked, with a painfully thoughtful expression on his face. "You are engaged to Paul. You're seriously going to get married next year?"
Lizzie was sitting at the table they had found on the street and painted blue; the paint was still sticky after four years. She had just picked up her coffee for a sip, but put it down for emphasis.
"January second is the day."
"Then if I asked you to come up to MoMA with me today you wouldn't be bothered if I said Neil was coming too."
It was just as he had imagined it would be. The coffee cup went back down, bang. Lizzie's face froze then her mouth gaped open; her nostrils began to quiver and turn red, her chin trembled and finally tears welled up and spilled out of her eyes. He felt a bit wicked watching all her self-assurance collapse like that, but also relieved to know Miss Sturm und drang was still alive and well.
Jonathan leaned against the doorway, a little amazed.
"Or maybe you would be bothered. Lizzie, it's been a long time. He doesn't know you might come, so don't."
"Why didn't you tell me last night? Why did he find you? When?"
"I didn't tell you last night because we don't hang out that much anymore and I wanted to fly around town, laugh, dance and drink with the Lizzie I knew, not the maudlin girl who used to ring me on the phone every Friday night when you were first on your own here in the city."
He walked over, took her chin in one hand and wiped tears from her cheek with the other.
"That's part of what you left behind as you woke up this morning, Lizzie. She's gone. Like it or not Mrs. Paul Tight-pants is awake and taking on the day in a black frock and stilettos at noon."
"Johnny, you are a heartless asshole and that is why I'll always love you."
"Thank you, I'm sure I love you the same way. Want a morning beer just to be trashy?"
"Nope, I don't think Dutch courage is what I require today."
Finally Lizzie took a sip of her coffee. "May I bum a smoke?"
Jonathan reappeared still naked, but with packet and lighter. He lit both cigarettes and passed one over to her shaky hand.

"It's been five years, right? You don't ditch someone for five years, excepting one postcard, if you really plan on asking them back, right?"
Fairly spitting the smoke out of his mouth, Jonathan shook his head, "Nope."
For about a year, Lizzie hadn't smoked, but now she sucked in all the fire with relish.
"One postcard from the Azores: No plan yet, N."
Jonathan had stood up and walked over to the stove to make another coffee.

"Johnny, that was right before you moved to the city and we got this place. God, that hurt." Lizzie fiddled the ashes off her cigarette and took a drag. "Still, it was the kick in the teeth I needed. But now here he is. It was bound to happen one day; I just wasn't expecting that day to be this one."
Next to the stove, Jonathan was still slowly pouring water through the filter, his bare bum turned toward her musings.
"Did he say why he was coming to town or was it one of those cryptic Neil messages?"
He glanced over his shoulder at her and back to the coffee. "On the Neil scale, I'd call it blunt. Continental Philosophy. Plan B. Arrive April 14. Tea and cakes?"
The last drips were falling into the pot and Jonathan stood transfixed by the tiny drops and ripples; his hand stayed fixed to the kettle, undecided.
"Oh. Hell. Neil."
Each syllable felt like a shiver rising up inside her and she reached for another smoke. As she lit it, Lizzie thought how naked her friend looked standing those few feet from her, goose bumps prickling blueish against his pale skin. He was studying the coffee as it poured into the cups, slouching down intently to measure out two equal portions.
"I e-mailed him my cell number... so he said he'd call around now... to meet up with me."
He said it then turned to her with the two cups and a smile.
"I'm going to vomit." Lizzie gave the fresh coffee a push, but the hot cup stuck to the paint and tipped.
"Because you no longer sleep with me, I no longer clean up your vomit,

so hurl at your own risk, but I'll get the coffee."

"How about some fresh air?"

"Quick coffee, clothes, meet you downstairs?"

"If I puke on the sidewalk no one has to clean it up – I love this city!" And Lizzie ran for the door.

She headed down the three flights of stairs feeling like they were moving beneath her feet, like she was at sea. The stale smoky smell was not helping the nausea so she tried rushing down the steps while clinging to the banister. Her heels pounded the tile floor as she ran for the door, out into the cold April sunshine. She'd forgotten her coat. Unable to face the stairs again, she shivered and pressed the intercom buzzer: Apt 3D.

"Johnny, it's me. I need my coat when you come down."

"And your purse and your watch and your wits. Down in a sec."

Jonathan was down in a flash, turned out in a combination of brilliant red corded jeans and funky flowered western shirt with a burgundy suede jacket they used to call the vomit coat, due to its personal history. In mock gallant fashion, he draped her leopard spot coat around her shoulders and fastened her watch on her wrist, kissed the hand, then closed it around the strap of her bag.

"We're off! He phoned and he's outside the Life Café."

Jonathan took her arm and they crossed the street, heading over to Avenue B, like they had done a million times before at every time of day and night. At the corner they turned down toward the park and even at that distance she could make him out, not where Jonathan was looking at the café, but across the street, watching them approach. Neil was waiting for the light to turn as they walked toward him. Lizzie didn't know what to do with her face. It was finding all these funny expressions it hadn't worn for years; half-smiles, one-sided pouting lip, quizzical eyebrows and it was moving in a familiar orchestrated interplay with his as he crossed E 10th St.

He'd grown up. His deeply tanned face had stronger lines, sharper cheekbones, an affected bit of stubble that was actually handsome as hell. The sun had done something to his eyes; they were pale and burned and burning. His hair had grown out and was now bleached a honey brown. It curled back from his face and hung round the collar of his pea coat.

By the time he reached her, Lizzie's head was cocked round, chin slightly tilted, looking rather like a funny blond and leopard-spot bird. Jonathan kept hold of Lizzie's hand, so Neil smiled at them both, crushed his cheek into Lizzie's and wrapped his arms tight around them both. Jonathan tossed his arms around his friends. He started to push them in a circle, half knocking them over until they began to spin with him in about five steps of a Russian dance, finally collapsing into the newspaper boxes at the curbside. In that one chaotic embrace, Lizzie felt years slip away; there was a visceral feeling of home that welled up in her heart and terrified her.

Jonathan tugged at his shirt collar and jacket, turned and smoothed Lizzie's hair, pretended to fix smudged lipstick and pinched her nose. Neil gave Jonathan one of his Humphrey Bogart looks and lines:
"If you'd told me you were bringing a lady with you, I'd 've gotten a hair cut, a proper shave."
And to Lizzie, "I believe we've met."
"I believe it was in Barcelona," she replied.
"If not this café? Then... ?" Jonathan asked pointing across the street to his favourite neighbourhood late breakfast spot.
"Wander!" Neil said in a mock sinister whisper.
"I vote west if we are possibly, eventually headed up to MoMA," Jonathan took the lead and pointed to the light showing green to cross the avenue.

They walked three abreast, arms linked, blocking the sidewalk and annoying the hurried people pushing past. They ambled, commenting on the dogs in the park, on yet another new restaurant in the damned restaurant corner. Neil seemed more familiar with New York than they would have guessed and after several cagey answers admitted that often a sailboat delivery would end with a free flight back to the States, so sometimes he booked a ticket with a layover in the city before heading down to Florida to start another job. He'd never looked up old friends because he didn't know what to say.

The city offers up so many faces that seem familiar at a distance, that make your heart race, you might follow someone for a few blocks thinking that when they turned a corner you would know for certain. Lizzie had done this more times than she wanted to remember, following a pea coat with a certain gait. Sometimes she would dream that it was him, stopping her with his smile and when she woke the next day she would find herself searching the streets with her eyes so that strangers stared back at her as if she had spoken to them. It was one of these days that she finally told Paul about Neil.

Paul had only known Lizzie a few weeks at that point, but watching the bizarre exchange of looks and clumsy wandering way she had that morning, he realised either something was wrong or she was totally mental. She didn't want to scare him away, but she still couldn't tell the story without falling to pieces. Was it mental? It wasn't just about losing some guy; it was about all the bad places she had put herself afterwards. How to say it? It was not exactly the most sparkling picture to paint for a serious new love.

They'd talked about it all in the end, that whole day, wandering around downtown. The blood and guts feeling of the ravaged World Trade Centre neighbourhood had suited their amblings. They still talked about Neil, about wounds that won't heal, about how to be crazy without being self-destructive, about how to love passionately not addictively. There were some great advantages to falling for a psychology specialist and the greatest advantage of all – that he cared because he seemed to love her absolutely. It still surprised her every day. But that was not what she was thinking about careening down 12th Street sandwiched between these two slices of her old life. They slowed down at the corner of Broadway and 12th to browse through the tables of books outside the Strand. Jonathan was flicking through a huge book of Weegee's photographs, eyeing the gruesome and pathetic street shots of New York in the forties. Neil was watching over his shoulder, wincing, sometimes laughing. Lizzie couldn't imagine five years had passed since they had all been together; it seemed so natural to be clowning around like this. She turned and started pawing through a pile of remaindered novels, reading first lines, seeing if their failings were advertised in first words.

When she felt his hands wrap around her shoulders, Lizzie jumped, then let herself be turned around to face the street. Neil's arm pressed against her cheek, outstretched, pointing to a green awning a few doors down. He whispered close into her other ear, "That diner."

She twisted her head to whisper back, which pressed her cheek into his, "The Bon Vivant is crap. I've eaten there."

She should have slapped him for all his physical presumption or just for buggering off for five years, but instead she held still between his insistent arm and stubbly cheek and remembered the time she thought she would spend her life here.

He whispered back "Not today! Today the food will be mediocre just the way a diner should be, not crap. Come on."

Lizzie gave Jonathan a 'what-the-hell-is-going-on-here?' look and followed Neil across the street.

They tucked into one of the booths by the window; then, shockingly, a waitress actually appeared bringing menus. She raised her eyebrows at Neil and looked across at Lizzie and Jonathan, "He looks just like the Old Spice Man, you know like just off a boat or something. You know?"

Her heavy Long Island accent was set off by a dramatic opera of facial expressions, followed by an attempt at whistling the tune.

"Coffee?"

All three just nodded, keeping mouths tight shut to hold back the laughter. The waitress again raised her eyebrows and left.

After regaining their composure, Lizzie and Johnny began peppering Neil with questions about where he'd been sailing and what plan had been represented so succinctly as "Continental Philosophy." Mid-conversation, Neil excused himself from the table to go smoke outside. The waitress chose that moment to come back to the table with coffee and to take their orders. Then she asked, "and for your husband?" This, directed at Lizzie.

"Two fried eggs, bacon, a toasted bagel with cream cheese. He's not my husband. I'm engaged, but not to him."

With hands on hips, the waitress replied, "No ring?"

"I left it at home because I was out... whatever." Lizzie gave a little wave of her hands.

"Oh, so you aren't Mrs. Old Spice? That's funny because you guys just seemed so ... I don't know. So together."

"We're not. We used to be. Could we end this conversation and get breakfast?"

"Sorry." Surly and Long Island make a bad combination in the word 'sorry'. Half way back to the kitchen, the waitress turned around and looked daggers at Lizzie,

"You know, this is just my day job. I'm the best psychic in Ronkonkoma." Lizzie looked at Jonathan and quickly hopped around to his side of the booth so she couldn't be seen from the direction of the kitchen. Slumping down to hide her hysterical shaking laughter, she covered her mouth, but then Jonathan snorted. She bit his sleeve trying not to howl out loud and finally stuffed her head in Jonathan's shoulder with tears streaming down her cheek. She didn't even see Neil slide back into his seat, but when she could breathe and open her eyes, he was staring back at her.

"You two look awfully cozy over there." He had tried to say it lightly, but his words had a sting to them.

Jonathan tried a quick change of subject, "Neil, you have the honour this morning of being served by a psychic, but she doesn't do breakfast orders, just relationships."

Lizzie couldn't help it; she took the bait and replied.

"After five years, that takes some crazy fucking gall!"

"What?"

"You can't sail off into the sunset and then show up one day and give me your jealousy crap."

"That was not jealousy; it was observation."

Neil was smiling a huge smile. Whatever had happened in the time they had been apart, a piece of her was still his. Old friends had told him about her being engaged. He had even spent a day in a café opposite Paul's apartment trying to get a glimpse of them together. When he'd seen Lizzie holding onto Paul as they left the building, he had thought he might want her back or at least to see that he could still have her. Despite disappearing for years, Neil had always imagined coming back sometime and imagined she would drop everything for him because she always had.

Lizzie's face was a little flushed, "OK, an observation."

And Jonathan chimed in, "Besides now she doesn't sleep with me anymore."

He laughed, but Lizzie kicked him under the table. She hoped Jonathan would correctly interpret the stiletto to ankle suggestion of silence.

"The convent was full when I moved to town," said Lizzie with raised eyebrows. In just a couple of hours she would return to her proper world, but for the moment she wanted a taste of what she had practised wanting for such a long time.

Laughing, Neil insisted, "Stop being prickly and eat your damn breakfast, Lizzie."

The waitress had just put Lizzie's plate down. Neil looked up at her and said,

"She actually is my wife; she simply doesn't approve of my smoking. And I did just get off a boat... all to commend your excellent service and psychic talents."

The waitress replied with a broad smile and promise of more coffee.

"You. Are. So. Bad!" Lizzie whispered after the waitress had left. The tense teasing continued through breakfast with Jonathan mostly listening, watching Lizzie melt back into a character he hadn't seen in years.

Many coffees later, they left the Bon Vivant and headed over to the flea market at 23rd St. It was late for any great deals, but they made their way to the vintage clothes and threw on each other, draped scarves, and chatted up the sellers. Neil disappeared for a moment and returned with a beautifully battered pair of cowboy boots; worn out black ostrich with multicoloured stitching.

He presented them to Lizzie, "Your feet are going to fall off if you keep hiking all over town in those heels. Put these on."

Leaning on his arm, Lizzie pulled off one shoe, handed it to Neil and pulled on the boot. "Perfect fit; now I'm really going to look like a lunatic."

She tucked her heels into her bag and glanced at her phone. Two texts from Paul.

Good morning, Sunshine! Hung? Followed by –*Surprise lunch invitation, later train. Meet at Tom and Sonya's?*

Normally she'd call to tell him about her evening and find out how his

talk had gone, but she almost couldn't imagine hearing his voice right now. Besides, she would interrupt
his lunch.
She sent a quick text –*See you there! Enjoy lunch, xLx*
"Paul?" Jonathan asked.
"Yup! I'm meeting him at eight," Lizzie said quickly.
"Paul?" asked Neil.
"Paul, Lizzie's fiancé Paul," Jonathan replied, smiling at Lizzie.
She bit her lip. She felt suddenly that she might be as crazy as she looked, fancy frock and boots, leopard spot coat, bed-head.
"Congratulations to you and the lucky gentleman." Neil gave her a slightly devilish grin.
Jonathan replied for Lizzie, "I like to call her Mrs Tight Pants or just "Itchy" for short, not shorts, but that's actually just me being mean. Paul's brilliant and adores Lizzie which is much more than I can say of some of her other city selections."
Lizzie shot back, "Nothing like friends; thanks Johnny. Shall we abandon our own artistic finds here and schlepp up to the Museum?"

They made their way to 53rd St and decided to split up for the visit. Jonathan had been planning to see a photo exhibit that only had a few days left, but Lizzie and Neil wanted to wander through the main collection. As Jonathan watched the two climb up the stairs away from him, he thought about the e-mails he and Neil had exchanged in the weeks before. He'd thought Lizzie needed a shake-up, just to see whether she had been changed by Paul or simply scared out of her chaos into a refuge that seemed about one size too small. He'd been amused that Neil wanted to see Lizzie, but without getting in touch with her first – his usual dramatic surprise. They had talked about a few different dates, but Neil had seemed keen to catch Lizzie after a night out. Only now something began to strike him as wrong; Neil's hand was in the small of her back pushing her up the stairs and she seemed unsure of where she was headed. Off-balance. That was it; by turning to look back at him, and his pushing her forward, Lizzie looked close to falling over.

Jonathan was tempted to follow them through the galleries, but instead headed off feeling vaguely annoyed with them both, with the exhibit, with himself. Two hours later, Jonathan tracked them down sitting on a bench in front of Edvard Munch's "The Storm", holding hands. And the clichéd "like an old couple" drilled into his mind, like they had weathered that storm together. Jonathan hadn't spent much time with Lizzie and Paul. Still he felt he would never see her melt into him that way. And still, it looked like capitulation, like defeat.

"Lizzie, it's almost five-thirty. The museum's closing. Let's head back downtown possibly for a drink?"

Jonathan had sat down on the opposite side of the bench and had leaned in, whispering to the back of Lizzie and Neil's heads.

"Sure," she said without turning around.

They followed Jonathan out of the room and slowly came out of their fog as they headed toward the doors of the museum.

Half an hour later they were all tucked into the back lounge of North Square – a late night place that felt a little louche so early in the evening.

"Martinis?" Neil proposed.

"No way, never again, not even with an olive," Lizzie was making a nasty face, but with a chortle underneath.

"Perfect. Jonathan? Martini?"

"I'll have what Lizzie's having."

"Excellent, three martinis. I'll go order them."

Neil left the table and Jonathan swooped in toward Lizzie, squeezing against her shoulder and pressing his cheek to her hair, "Is this what you want?"

"This is what I wanted for ages and now it's just what I want until eight o'clock."

She reached over, grabbed his hand and gave him a mischievous smile.

In most instances this would have been the secret signal between them that everything was under control, but it felt hollow to him. Jonathan fixed his eyes on the far corner of the table, "Lizzie, I like Paul more now."

"What does that mean?"

He wrapped both his hands around hers and stared down at them.

"I wanted you to stay with me in the zone of chaos. I get lonely spinning out of control on my own, but that's not you anymore and never made you really happy. I thought you were giving in to convention and all that bullshit: marriage, kids, work, early mornings, at least I don't foresee sensible shoes. But looking at how you are with Paul, I see a really strong woman– a little nipped in at the edges maybe, but independent. And today, you..."

"Three martinis it is then. Thanks, Neil." Lizzie was giving Jonathan a determined 'not now thank you' look.

All three knocked back their drinks too quickly and Neil fetched three more. Diving into her next cocktail, Lizzie realised she wouldn't have time to go home and change for dinner and that she would irritate Paul by turning up tipsy.

Neil started telling them about the boat he had borrowed to live on September through May. He would make some repairs and maintain it while living cheaply at some mooring on the Sound, not too far from his school. There it was – their plan – only now she wasn't in it. Jonathan started grilling Neil about his thesis proposals so that by the time they were talking Bergson and memory, Lizzie could lean back into the banquette and feel the gin tingling through her. Melting into Neil's plans and life had been not unlike gin, taken early in the morning as well as at night. Now she never felt that way. Being loved could still be part of being alone or even lonely, just loved from the outside. Her mind drifted through images of walls and water.

"One more or shall we go?" It was Jonathan, asking while pulling on his coat.

Then, Neil eyeing the bar and pulling out his wallet said, "I'm staying for another. Lizzie?"

"How about some water and a tea?" Lizzie was hoping that would put her up on her feet in the next twenty minutes before she walked back into a world where she wouldn't wash away.

With a quick kiss and squeeze, Jonathan left as Neil headed back with two more martinis.

Lizzie laughed, "If I drink this I will fall over and be unable to move."

"Go ahead."

"I can't."

"Don't want to?"

"Can't."

"Want to?"
"Tell me about the boat."

Neil leaned into her and began telling her how this guy in the Greek Isles had asked him to take some friends around for a few weeks while he flew back to the States on business. It had been a roaring success and they had kept in touch and finally the offer of off-season maintenance had sprung up. It was unlikely and unreasonable, but that was Neil all over; everything fell into his hands.

Now Neil's hand was wrapped around hers on the table. Lizzie's gaze drifted to his watch. The meaning of the hands sifted into her mind and she jumped, "I'm late!"

"I'll walk you there."

"No, really. It's around the corner."

"Come on, Lizzie. I'll make sure you get up the right stairs."

He took her chin in his hand and pushed his thumb to tilt it up.

She dove down to collect her bag from the floor. The martinis had gone to her head and all she could think of was Alice in Wonderland, that perhaps she could fall into her handbag and find herself in a world beneath her own where maybe she could try the Mad Hatter's tea party before heading back to her dinner party.

Then Neil's face was down by the leg of her chair smiling and rattling, "Oh dear! Oh dear! I shall be too late."

There he was: her white rabbit. Under the table was already halfway down the rabbit-hole.

May | London
Miranda Glover

In magazine offices down London backstreets skin-tight girls were waking to a routine Susie used to share. They prepared to skim cream off life's surface and churn it into glossy copy for consumption by millions of women who aspired to be, but were not quite like them. Each weekday morning they crawled from random beds – habitually not their own – in the thick, airless folds of the city, and tripped in their offbeat clothes to the nearest underground station.

In daylight, subtle features set one apart from the next; a copper-coated ring from 'travels in Brazil', an unexplained tree-like scar down the inside of a wrist, a lilt to an accent that hinted at foreign blood. As they waited on fuggy platforms, these bright young things dug deep inside overstuffed handbags, past lipsticks, spare underwear and trial-size perfumes, to retrieve their sacred BlackBerries. They checked texts for the night ahead, sent cryptic messages to conquests from the night before. Creaking tubes pulled in with a rush of warm air and they squeezed on with a grimace, pushing their iPods to play.

Susie stood in Kensington Gardens. Her reflection rippled in the black water that filled the ornamental pools. Beneath her clothes her limbs were still bed-warm. Only her breasts remained taut, brimful with milk for Cara. The baby was sleeping at last, tightly swaddled in her buggy. Susie wouldn't wake her to relieve the throbbing. She'd been submerged with her daughter since dawn. Tom had taken to the sofa bed in the lounge. Now she'd emerged into the park to swallow her own sustenance; the fresh morning air. She shivered unexpectedly under the ruffled sky. May, it was late May, springtime in London, yet a spike of cold snaked its way down her spine, reminding her of winter. Blurred events threw a momentary shadow across her mind.

Spray spurted unannounced from the fountains, sprinkling faint ripples over the inky pools. With its sound, like gravel hitting ice, the city forced its way back into her senses. It was still there, all about her: London. Along the Bayswater Road and across the park traffic squealed and groaned. Cara stirred and Susie pushed the buggy back and forth, looking vacantly towards the Serpentine, glinting sharply beneath a moment's sunshine. She dropped sunglasses over her eyes as someone passed so close behind her that she felt the swish of cloth. Swinging round, she watched as a woman in a long, black coat hurried away from the pools, then down towards the river. Susie wondered at her age. She was tall, like Susie, yet finer-boned, as her mother had been. Susie thought momentarily. Was she, herself, thirty or thirty-one now? It was hard to remember details like that today. Spontaneously, she turned the buggy and followed in the woman's footsteps.

Meanwhile, the girls had arrived at their magazine offices, corrected their telling faces in staff toilets, made instant black coffee, switched on computers and checked mail. At morning meetings caffeine-enhanced anxiety bristled on their skin as editors threw razor-sharp eyes over their latest copy. Every magazine had one – a forty-something female with a pinched waist, face and life, a queen bee who had eschewed the babymaking machine and triumphantly stayed her professional ground. They were a rarer breed than the former Susie-clones; the one out of a hundred who had not succumbed to the internal clock. At once the twenty-somethings admired yet loathed her; she was a source of constant self-comparison and undisclosed fear – unlike the male publishers whom they simply accepted were in charge of their pay, but not their emotions. The editors knew by instinct when you had spent the night shagging a stranger, snorting cocaine, or drinking until you nearly drowned. They knew if you'd taken a short cut on copy, fallen out with the ad' manager, or, even worse, a PR. And they always made you pay.

Through her, these younger women had learned to be ruthlessly ambitious and to hold no prisoners of their own. They kept stabbing knives in their desk drawers for competing females' backs, swallowed diet pills, drank coke zero and smoked Camel Lights to remain emaciated and employed. They swore allegiance to their queen: when she spoke they took notes, when she moved they took notes, but when she breathed, they held their breaths. On the sly they sent texts to friends, arranged cheap weekends in Prague, shopped online for deviant treats. And then they wrote copy, thousands of words of copy about beauty, celebrity and the balance for which all women strive. It was a subject about which they thought they knew ample, but as most would learn later, they in fact knew nothing, nothing at all.

Susie had been one of them and she had loved her life; the constant stream of ideas, of parties, of freebies. She had thought they provided words of wisdom – ha! She had thought they made some sense – ha! These ruminations surfaced in time with her quickening step. The woman moved so fast, yet so effortlessly, as if, under that long, dark coat, her feet were floating above the path. Those girls in their magazines were where she had been, thought Susie – sitting inside a nest of thorns, unaware that their inevitable flights would end in despair. She felt a rush of blood to her head; 'despair' – the word was out. It had spoken itself aloud. She had spoken it aloud. There! She held it on her tongue, then exhaled it with her fastening breath, repeated it over and again.

She was moving even more quickly now, hastening Cara's buggy before her, until one of the wheels veered off the path and lifted the whole contraption at an angle. Susie slowed. She wouldn't take Cara with her off the rails. Her pace slowed more and then she stopped. The figure was moving into the middle distance. Susie watched until it was out of sight. It was as if the force of her passing by had lifted Susie into her jet stream and triggered this self-confession. She had to face it: she was drowning.

Susie made her way back to the ornamental pools. Despite the sudden movements, Cara continued to sleep. She would sit for a moment, on a park bench, she decided. And then she would go home for lunch.

Morning meetings done, in the magazine offices the girls went back to their desks to send more e-mails, call journalists and set up photo shoots. They had a list of stories to work on; *The Double Duty Wardrobe,*

Anti-Ageing Makeover, 23 Ways to Survive an Affair. They would have to find real life stories to fit inside these ideas, to qualify them, to make them read true. And they had to remember that even though it was early summer now, they were working on the November issue. They had to think darkening days, turning leaves, Halloween ghouls and bonfire nights. They sat down and concentrated, forgot about their private lives. This was the time of day when their brains began to work.

Susie sat on the park bench in a daze. Still there was nobody in the gardens. It amazed her, how quiet it was here in the mornings. Until she'd had Cara she'd never given a thought to the weekday life of the city; acres of meandering parkland, the whispering side rooms of public art galleries, museum corridors where little stirred but dust. Now she was familiar with their ghostly quiet. Kensington Gardens was one of those places. Generally she found herself alone here, although occasionally she'd see another lost soul, someone who looked old or infirm, or another novice outsider, like her.

She and Tom only lived two streets away from the park. They'd bought their tiny flat before Cara came. It had suited them; they liked jogging, walking to Kensington for art-house movies and spicy Thai food on early summer evenings. It wasn't so easy now, with the buggy. They were three floors up and if Susie left it in the foyer the neighbours got upset. Getting Cara in and out of the flat was a daily challenge. She had first to put her in her cot, then take the folded buggy down the stairs, come back up for the baby and then bring her down, reversing the process on coming home. She didn't like to be separated from Cara, even for a few moments. What if she choked or rolled over and fell out of the cot? Susie hadn't yet allowed anyone else to take care of her, apart from Tom, of course, but he worked so much that the days felt very long when she was here alone. She felt removed from him. They seemed to be growing apart, Cara between them like a mental block. She glanced at her watch. Still only 11.45am. If she were at work the day would only just be getting going. Now the hours until Tom came home moved in slow motion. Sometimes she found herself counting the minutes. She felt a moment's panic. Six months' leave. How would she concentrate on anything else, ever again?

"She's very young."
Susie jumped. She hadn't heard anyone approach but standing next to her now was the woman in the long dark coat. She'd reappeared as silently and unexpectedly as before; as if she'd floated in from out of the blue. She was looking down into the buggy. Late middle-aged, very pale skin, fading brown hair shot through with silver, pinned at the knape of her neck. Older than her own mother had been. The woman tilted her head and surveyed Susie surveying her. She had a certain, intent smile and dark, penetrating eyes. There was something familiar about her. For a moment Susie wondered if she were a famous actress. She could be a Redgrave, she thought. Had that hauteur about her; a stage presence; a deportment that raised her slightly above the ordinary.

The woman sat down next to Susie and placed her hands one over the other. Her fingers were long, thin and bloodless. Free of rings. Cara stirred, then she began to cry. Susie's breasts prickled.
"She needs a feed," she murmured, lifting the baby gently from the buggy and cradling her on her lap. She began to wrestle uneasily with the clip on her feeding bra. Cara turned her head towards the left breast and opened her mouth frantically, in a fishlike sucking motion.
"Pass her to me while you arrange yourself," the woman said.
Her voice was clipped, and coated in authority. Mechanically Susie handed Cara into her arms. Immediately the baby ceased to wriggle.
"She can't smell the milk now," the woman added, eyeing Susie sideways.

Susie retrieved a shawl from underneath the buggy, put it around her shoulders. The woman handed Cara back gently and Susie latched her on. The baby fed frantically at first, then more calmly as her hunger was relieved.

Across town the girls began to glance at their computer clocks. Their attentions were waning. An hour and a half had passed since they'd sat down at their screens. Time for a skinny latte and naked crayfish salad. They left their desks in twos and threes, casting discreet glances into soundproofed glass rooms where their editors skipped lunch in preference for control. Then they took the office lifts down to street level.

"He said he wanted a picture of me," said one, as the coffee machine in Starbucks clunked, "to see how I looked, you know, in digital."

"In digital?" her friend enquired as she stirred chocolate into the fat-free froth.

"My tits," the first murmured, "so he could admire them while he worked."

She passed her phone over with a smirk.

"How did you take it?"

"In the work toilets with my back to the door, pulled up my T-Shirt and clicked."

"Not bad for an amateur, but it's more soft porn than Mario Testino."

"'Fraid he was too busy this morning to be of assistance to me."

They giggle and think they are funny and young and cool and emancipated, taking photos of their unstretched bodies for their latest lovers to fantasise over.

"Are you sure he won't use it to blackmail you one day?"

"I'm not that special, who would care?"

"Your kids might, one day."

"Hmm, if I ever get round to having any...."

"Well I wouldn't do it," the other girl said. "I mean, you know I'm not a prude, but I don't think I'd send photographs like that. They're in the public domain. What if he showed them to someone else?"

"Says Ms Morality who had a zipfuck with her boss last week."

"Shhh, someone might hear."

The girls leave their lurid conversations and styrofoam cups inside the coffee bars and return to their desks. The editors note their arrivals through the glass walls. It was no good to take more than your share of the hour; forty minutes was acceptable, any more implied a lack of true duty. And then the afternoon began: a rush of ideas and writing and phone calls until five thirty – and even then there was no getting around the sense of pride in overtime, unpaid but expected, if you were really serious about your future. Which, of course they all were. Some wanted to make it from style to features, others from subbing to full production. It was one big buzz. They all wanted to rise up the masthead to a position of authority. They thought it was their shared ambition, their goal. To be eventually where she was, that queen with the sting in her tail. They didn't really think about family life and having children; seemed somehow not right for them, definitely not now. They were too busy influencing the zeitgeist to consider going towards a future on the other side.

�֍

"My children left me a long time ago, now," the woman said to Susie. "When they were babies I used to walk with them here in the mornings. I've seen you, before, looking into the pools. I used to watch the water too. I'd see my face shimmering there like a picture, and think, 'Who is that woman who used to be me?'"

Susie listened drowsily. It was always this way when she fed Cara. She lost the tension. Between feeds it would build back up, like a damn fit to burst. And then Cara would take the milk and her breasts would soften, her mind become a blank. Sometimes tears came at that point, and she remembered her mother.

"I would walk around for hours, but back in those days a woman couldn't be seen to feed her child in public," she continued. "So I'd have to go back home. It's much better this way. The open air and spaces keep your mind lucid. These early months can be quite lonely, unless you live inside a large family."

"No one seems to any more," Susie murmured. "Tom, he's always at work and there isn't anyone else. They're all away."

"I remember thinking; where do I go from here?" rejoined the woman. "I thought my life had come to an end. All I saw ahead was a big, cold, misted window, with me pressing my nose up against it; the children holding onto my legs, holding me back, and I'd think; their future is my loss."

"Did you work, before the children?" Susie asked.

"I studied art, at Chelsea, then I assisted a sculptress. Over there, just by the palace. She was very unusual for her class, a talented woman driven by her art. I married a man who worked for her mother, as a driver.

Gerald. I was smitten before I ever heard his name. We had no need for me to work after the children came along. Gerald would come back for lunch and then he would go back to work again, often until quite late in the evenings. He wasn't an unkind man, but with age he lost the art of conversation. Or maybe he just lost it with me. We would always retire together and sometimes he would want me, you know, in that way, and then we'd sleep. But we rarely talked. I of course was so tired from the constant demands of the children that I needed sleep too. But we should've found a way to talk."

"We're always too tired now, for conversations," replied Susie, "About anything but Cara."

"Time passes so fast. In the case of my children, two grew well, but sadly Beth, the youngest, didn't make it past her third year. Suddenly the other two were older and began to leave me in subtle physical and emotional ways. It was only when they'd gone I realised how much I had loved it, every second of it; of their growing and how in some ways it had all been mine, exclusively mine, even the moments like this, when I was melancholic, sitting on a park bench in Kensington Gardens, wondering who I was, with Charlotte or Kit or Beth sleeping next to me in their prams. Suddenly those moments seemed not empty, but brimful with life. And I wished for it all over again."

"Really?" the word escaped from Susie's lips.

"Oh yes. Embrace your daughter, enjoy her, Susie. And make sure you talk to Tom. It was the dusking hours that filled me with particular dread. Find a way to enjoy them. Now. They won't last forever."

Susie felt the slowing of Cara's suck, then the baby's milk-softened lips fell away from her breast. She turned her over to wind her, rubbing Cara's back, round and round until she felt her hiccup against her heart.

"Thank you," she said. "I feel better."

The woman sat looking towards the pools.

"Your mother, I'm sure she loves her too," she said.

There was a wisdom about her. Susie wasn't afraid of it. Her words were true and clean and lacking in spin.

"She's, she's not with us any more."

"Well then you must love her twice as much for the both of you."

Susie had lost Alice only weeks before Cara arrived. They all knew that it was coming, her end. But why did it have to be before she'd even met her granddaughter? It seemed so cruel, such a slight, for them all. She rose and put Cara back in the buggy and held onto the handles. The woman rose too.

"You look pale. You need something sweet before you walk home. Here."

Her long, thin hand slid inside her coat pocket and she pulled out a tiny glass jar and a silver teaspoon.

"When the children were infants Gerald set up the Royal Honey Company. Imagine it, London honey from hives on the top of the royal rooftops and from inside the Royal Parks, too. From Kensington Palace, Buckingham Palace, Hyde Park and St James's – and of course from Kensington Gardens. I always keep a small pot in my pocket, for moments like this. Have a spoonful."

Susie dipped the tiny silver spoon into the pot and put the honey in her mouth. It slipped easily down her throat. As it settled inside her, a deep warmth began to surge upwards from her centre. It stretched her face back into the most enormous smile. It took Susie aback, this sudden, unbridled elation that seemed to spring from the place inside her where, for months, Cara had grown. And now she wasn't just smiling but laughing and the woman was laughing too.

✤

"How about *Ethereal Evenings*," suggests the assistant fashion editor. "You know – the colours and the atmosphere are ghostly; it feels Victorian, like a wisp of memory."

"*Wisp of Memory*, I like that better, or in fact, *Wisps of Memory*, yes even better still," replies the editor. "And we'll use that image of the model in the long, black gown on the cover. She looks like a spirit, running free through the park with all that red hair. I think the photographer's done a great job. Who was it?"

"Chris, Chris Jones. Yeah, it's true, she looks unworldly, in that black gown, and I love the water shimmering behind her – the sun's turning the edges of her hair scarlet – great for autumn."

Today, for once, the assistant fashion editor is on a creative roll and seems to be on the right side of the editor.

"Where was the shoot taken?"

"Kensington Gardens. Chris suggested it. He'd been reading about Queen Victoria's daughter, Princess Louise. Apparently she was a talented artist. She made that sculpture of Victoria in the park. She had an assistant, a woman, whose daughter drowned in the water pools. Story goes she's haunted them ever since, gazes into the water, searching for her child. Perfect story for Halloween! We took some shots there. Look."

"What's that smudge, in the background of that one? Is that a mark on the image?"

The assistant fashion editor's heart begins to thump.

"No, I think it's someone walking... yes it is. Look, it's a woman in a long, dark coat – I think it adds to the picture; she almost looks like she's floating."

The queen bee takes a forensic look, then agrees and the assistant fashion editor is relieved. She'd just made that bit up; about the woman on the path. Chris had screwed up, the smudge was unintentional. She'd hoped the editor wouldn't notice it, but when she looked at it again now, it did look like a bit like a figure. She liked it there, and everything else about the picture was perfect. They could always Photoshop the smudge out, but now she was looking at it again, it seemed to add to its haunting quality. However much you tried to construct an image, sometimes it was the unexpected that really made it work.

Susie turned and she pushed the buggy out of Kensington Gardens, towards the Bayswater Road. The feeling of elation stayed with her. In her mind she began to think forwards, into a future where Cara was a toddler, a child, a teenager, a young adult woman, and she felt a surge of anticipation. It was all there to look forward to. She would do it for herself, and for Alice too. As she reached the exit she turned. The woman was still there, standing by one of the octagonal pools, gazing into the water. It was only then Susie realised she still held her delicate silver spoon. The handle was engraved with a chain of daisies. On the back was the name Beth. She needed to give it back. Susie turned Cara's buggy around. She looked around the pools, but there was no sign of the woman. Surely she could not have moved so far or so fast, even if she had gone, again, at a pace.

A gardener was there now, sweeping litter up from between the benches. Susie hadn't noticed him earlier, but it had to be worth a shot.

"Excuse me, did you see," she asked, gesturing towards the bench, "which way she went, the woman who was talking to me?"

The man surveyed her, quizzically.

"I saw you sitting there, Miss," he said, "Just now."

"Yes," Susie reasserted. "And the woman. Did you see where she went?"

He looked quizzical.

"Sorry, love, no. I saw you though. You were sitting right there, feeding your baby. But I never saw no one else – you were definitely on your own."

"You look amazing!" says the assistant fashion editor. "How's that lovely baby?"

Susie's standing in the middle of the air-conditioned room. The strip-lighting feels foreign and she'd forgotten that slightly paper and polish smell that offices always have.

"She's lovely, we're doing fine," says Susie. "I can't believe she's already five months old."

As she says it a spring uncoils inside Susie and she smiles. She feels brave and relieved and very well. She's left Cara with Tom for the morning, while she comes into work, so she can concentrate. They'd talked about it, she and Tom, over and over during the past few months. He'd been patient and understanding, that she didn't feel it was right, to be a full-time working mum while Cara was small. She'd freelance to make a bit of money, try to write some more grown-up stuff. She felt wiser, since having Cara, more aware of how things really were.

"Have a look at the November issue, it's just come in," enthuses the assistant fashion editor.

Susie takes the copy from her. On the cover is a model with flaming red hair, running through the Italian water gardens.

"That's where I go with Cara every day," exclaims Susie. "I can't believe," then she stops, looks at the picture more closely.

"What?" asks the assistant fashion editor. "Don't tell me you've spotted an error, she'll kill me."

"No," says Susie. "No it's just the figure, in the background. She looks like someone I met once in the park. It sounds silly, but she gave me some honey and left before I had a chance to give her back her spoon... and I haven't seen her since."

The assistant fashion editor opens her mouth to speak, just as the editor appears and kisses the air each side of Susie's cheeks.

"You look amazing, Susie," she gushes, glancing momentarily over her baby-thickened waist. "Now I have just ten minutes. Shall we have a quick chat?"

Susie mouths, 'speak to you later' and follows the editor into her office. She knows her next words are predictable and expected, that the editor is not surprised to hear her say 'goodbye'.

When it's over she returns to the assistant fashion editor's desk. Her chair's empty. She's left a note, stuck on her screen: "*S - had to go to a shoot - call me!*"

Susie screws the note into a ball and throws it in the bin. She knows she won't call; their friendship had just been a work thing. And now she has to go. Cara needs her feed. She picks up the cover proof, puts it in her bag and hastens towards the lift, then happily presses to go to ground.

June | Amsterdam
Anne Tuite-Dalton

It was barely nine in the morning and they had already passed through customs.

"I'll take your bag mum," said Juliette.

Catherine smiled at her daughter, "Thanks, I won't be a minute."

The slight teenager took the small case's handle and, rolling her own one alongside it, walked away from the main stream of hurried travellers towards an empty space along the wall. Catherine disappeared into the ladies' loo. Large tulips were painted on the cubicle door. In an hour or so they would be in the heart of Amsterdam.

Catherine had visited the Dutch city with two friends after completing her law degree; twenty years ago. She had enjoyed those few days very much, remembered long evenings spent going from one coffee house to another, and a Dutch man she'd met – his name began with an H she thought, the beer they'd drunk and the cycle trip to Keukenhof Gardens: the sea of colours had taken her breath away, especially the reds and the yellows. She wondered whether those tulips would have looked so bright back then had Jonathan been with her. She was looking forward to spending this weekend with her daughter – and without him. It was only a few hours since their separation and yet it already seemed distant.

Despite a missing hairbrush, a passport at the bottom of a suitcase and a last minute dash for an extra key, they'd arrived at the airport with a bit of time to spare. The four of them had gone to a terminal café for coffee, orange juice and croissants.

"It's been a long time since we've all had breakfast together." said Jonathan.

The comment was characteristically loaded. Catherine had long learned not to react.

"Louis, get off! It's mine." Juliette had shrieked, pulling on a bit of croissant with one hand and whacking her brother on the arm with the other.

Louis and Juliette had exchanged more harsh words, both trying to outdo the other, then Juliette had stuck her tongue out at him, straight, pointy, dark red and fleshy. Catherine had a sudden vision of metal studs on it. The less gory reality brought a sense of relief and she'd decided to keep quiet about the emerald gloss covering Juliette's nails.

"Enough, just stop it you two," she finally reprimanded, loudly. She had so wanted this departure to be free of confrontation. Jonathan had remained quiet, slightly distanced from the situation.

"OK kids, time to go," he said flatly, turning to Catherine.

They'd got up, gathered their stuff and kissed goodbye. All that Catherine received from her husband was a peck on the cheek, no more no less than the kids. And then they'd all gone their separate ways.

When Catherine emerged from the Ladies she spied Juliette, still guarding the suitcases, immobile in the flow of hurried passengers. She was looking down at her phone, her fingers nimbly typing away. She was so absorbed she wasn't conscious of Catherine's watching eyes.

Ya with Val?

What ya doing tonight?...

Lucky...

Yeah, I hope, will tell ya all.

Not sure.

Then she'd glanced up and noticed her mother, scowled and typed hurriedly.

POS

Miss ya loads xxxx

"POS?" asked Catherine teasingly.

Juliette shrugged.

Outside Central station, blue and white trams came and went regularly; it was easy to find the right one. Twenty minutes later, they alighted and left the main road, a large artery pulsing rhythmically with the flux and reflux of trams, and entered a narrow street. A distinct and strong smell of grass was floating in the air, and around the corner a few tables and chairs invited passers by to sit down. Further up the street a small white shop front caught their eye.

"How weird mum, it says 'hospital' in purple letters!"
They both looked through the opaque, white glass; a middle aged woman, wearing a short, red dress and long, tall, red patent boots was standing in the middle of the room, talking to a man behind the counter. Another younger woman wearing jeans sat in a corner and they could make out the bald head of a man, leaning against the window.
"A waiting room, probably a surgery, Dutch style," replied Catherine walking on.

The hotel was a street or two away. When they arrived, the man in the lobby was friendly, handsome too in an understated way. He had a curious mark above his right eyebrow; it was green, the size and shape of a coffee bean.
"Did you 'ave a good trip?"
His body was slightly turned towards Catherine and he was clearly addressing her: room number, details about breakfast, keys, tramway routes. His eyes, however, kept wandering back to Juliette. She feigned indifference, leaning against the wooden counter, her slender arm resting on the polished and worn surface, casually flicking through a brochure. Whenever Catherine spoke, however, her eyelids lifted carefully. Catherine noticed the silent game and was slightly irritated by Juliette's dismissive air.
"All right Juliette, I think we have all the information we need. Let's go up."
"Mum you're, like, just, just so embarrassing."
"What did I do?" asked Catherine.
"You were just so rude to him, he was still talking to you when you told me we should go up."
"Oh don't worry," Catherine replied spiritedly, determined not to descend into a row. "He won't have noticed. Now room number ... thirty-three."

The door opened easily into a bright space, twin beds and a view over the hotel's overgrown back gardens. They had not shared a room together for a long, long time and Catherine was excited at the thought of being in such close quarters with her daughter. There might be giggles and late night chats. Juliette tended to be the one in control of the tone of their relationship now. A year or so before she had decided to take a slight step back: all of her jokes, hugs and attempts at any kind of intimacy were thrown back to her with the speed of a boomerang. They still had fun together, every so often Juliette was affectionate or asked for help and advice but it was all on her terms. With a pinch of regret for the little girl who used to sit on her lap demanding hugs, Catherine was determined to accept her daughter's newly found independence but it wasn't always easy to get the balance right.

"Should we try cycling, Juliette?"

"Not sure. Those cyclists, they're, like, very good."

"All right it might be more relaxing to go on foot then. And I noticed a leaflet yesterday about pedalos. We could try that later."

"Yep, whatever." Catherine bit her lip and ignored Juliette's curt reply, and the fact that she was looking down at her phone, again.

They emerged from the hotel an hour later. The morning was blue with a tinge of yellow, the sunlight finding its way past the tall roofs, seeping through the green of the young leaves. It was warm too, a perfect day for walking around a city. They tried to stick to the part of the pavement that was allocated to pedestrians, at times crossed over the white line and once or twice had to hold on to each other as a bike swerved past them at full speed. By the end of the weekend, hopefully, they'd get used to it all.

Catherine and Juliette crossed a small market square with a large sand-coloured church in the centre. Opposite them, in a corner, stood the museum; similar, but not identical to another townhouse. The typical panelled windows and frames had been replaced by pure glass, making the windows taller and wider and giving the house a modern look.

They joined the almost static, long line of people slithering its way around the corner to the entrance facing the canal. Once in a while, the queue moved, slowly. Catherine and Juliette were waiting; waiting, along with hundreds of others, to see the house where a young girl had herself waited for months in the hope that her normal life was going to resume. The queue was strangely subdued, a sense of awe rippled through the visitors, they felt the sanctity of the place, of the pavement they were treading. They knew the story; it had begun with a name – Anne Frank – and finished with a number, random yet unique, tattooed on her wrist. That story belonged to history, to a past that was taught in classrooms around the world. But the diary also belonged to their own past, to the moment in their lives when childhood had been left behind.

Catherine looked at her daughter, standing there, pensive. "Are you ok, Juliette?" she asked gently.

"I'm all right. I can't believe I'm, like, here. I read bits of the book again last week."

Catherine checked herself. Her daughter, who was always so detached so cool these days was visibly moved.

The doors finally opened in front of them and they were in, each room a new stage for a drama that had unfolded long ago. A life that had ended in a camp.

When they came back outside the sun was high in the sky, the morning light had turned to a strong blue. They walked along the canal, silently, their steps in tune. The waterways, their regularity, broken by the trees bordering them, brought a sense of relief. Tall, long, elegant houses stood on the sides seemingly looking at their city. Amsterdam was calm, dignified. They stood on a bridge. Catherine and Juliette both looked down, into the water running underneath them. The sunrays mirrored them: Juliette's blond hair, her dark T-shirt, Catherine's light tunic, her face a cream oval. Fragile images.

"It's interesting isn't it how we are defined by how others see us, by the vision they have of us. And this image is very important to all, especially teenagers."

"Yes and..." Juliette replied, slightly impatiently maybe. Catherine carried on unperturbed.

"Well, for instance Anne Frank, stuck in this small space with all these people, was aware of her image, of how these others saw her. With her diary she was able to bring some distance between her and the image of herself that she got back from them. Somehow she managed to carve herself a new identity. She did that in peace, alone, away from any influence."

"And so??"

"Well it is very different from what you do today, with Facebook and all those other ways you have to communicate constantly with each other."

"Yeah, but her diary, now we can all read what she wrote, about being in love with Peter, about the silly arguments they all had..."

"Yes but it started as something quiet and blank to lay her thoughts on and it's only become public because of the circumstances."

"Well she wanted to be a writer, so it might be she was really writing for, like, an audience."

Their steps carried them further on. Along the way, barges – messy ones, with old bits of bikes and other bric-a-brac littering the deck, some covered in plants, others immaculately bare. It was easy to get a glimpse of life

onboard: someone making coffee, someone else reading on a chaise longue, in public, but apparently unfazed.

To Catherine, there seemed to be no line, no distance between the private space these people lived in and the outer world, looking in, hovering nearby. She felt vulnerable on their behalf. Catherine looked at her daughter, her hair, long and smooth, reflected the sunlight. She tried to remember what it felt like being sixteen. She turned away carefully. A man was pushing his bike off a plank, such a public display of movement.

"To me your Facebook is like living on one of these."

"What do you mean mum?"

"Well Facebook leaves you just as exposed as they are."

Juliette was quiet for a while and then said, "Weird, weird mum, not sure about what you're saying."

"Well think about it Juliette. What you do, what you think, what you like and who you like, who you hang out with and where you go is in there, isn't it? All of it. There's no borderline between you and those who want to know what you're up to. Your are open, transparent, like glass."

Juliette looked ahead, clearly puzzled, thinking. "I guess you're kind of right, but I only, like, give what I want to give."

"Yes but you give a lot away and once out, you can't take it back. The image of your life, those bits you give, do you never wish you'd kept them to yourself?"

"Well they're me, like, they are just... so me; so no, I, I don't mind. You know nothing about it, really. I don't know where I'd be without Facebook. You're, like, so old-fashioned."

The mother turned to her daughter. "Old fashioned... I suppose in a way I am. It's just that..." She was not sure she would find the right words.

"Go on mum, tell me what's on your mind."

"Well what your friends, your generation, you can get out of Facebook seems just very superficial to me. It's all so public and it all happens in an environment which is distant from you, so I can't see really how you can get anything constructive out of it. It all seems so ... unreal."

"Not that unreal, it's a site for friends, remember?" asked Juliette.

Phoney. Catherine thought.

"Friends. Maybe, but you hardly know any of them or do you? And it seems to me," Catherine carried on, "that you control that image, you change it, you experiment with it to the point when it's not really you anymore."

"Guess so. But it's all very friendly and it's fun and it feels good to belong to this, like, kinda club."

"Maybe, but to me the publicity of it all is uncomfortable, threatening even."

A broken mirror, each piece revealing a bit of her daughter, that's what Catherine had in mind when she thought of Facebook.

"Ok. Well, like dad says, let's agree to disagree." Catherine was surprised, usually Juliette did not let go of an argument.

They pedalled their way through a maze of canals. The pushing was slow and powerful. Their feet, their whole bodies worked against the strong pressure of the water, but they could let their minds wander and it suited the leisurely mood of the town. People were ambling about on their boats, on the bridges, cyclists were coming and going in all directions. The Amsterdamers went about their business in a relaxed manner, the clothes they wore showed their informal yet stylish attitude to life.

Back at the hotel, the man with the little coffee bean as a third eye, was pottering about, his dark skin in sharp contrast with his blond hair.

"Hi, is everythink ok?"

"Yes thank you."

His eyes were fixed on Juliette's.

"By de way, my name is Sjap. 'ave a good day?"

"We saw Anne Frank's house and the Rijkmuseum."

"And tomorrow? Wat will you see?"

"Not sure yet. The Van Gogh museum... and do some shopping."

"Nice. If you need any 'elp please ask me."

As they made their way upstairs, Catherine noticed Juliette's legs; the smooth, taught skin behind the knee. The expression on her face had changed too, she'd recently developed a tendency to pout. Since the braces had been removed after Christmas and in tempo with the arrival of spring, Juliette had blossomed. The years had brought more flesh, more curves and Catherine had observed the changes. Now though, for the first time, she also sensed Juliette's sexuality.

"Mum, what's that? Is that, like, a dress or a long shirt?"

Juliette was bent over the desk, her mascara held frozen in mid air, her face almost touching the mirror, looking away from her own reflection at the figure of her mum standing behind her.

"Well, a long shirt, a tunic I think. Why, don't you like it?"

"Just a bit shapeless and, like, weird colour. But fine, it's fine." End of conversation, she was now carefully blackening her eyelashes.

Catherine suddenly felt unsure, the tunic that had looked so right in the shop seemed a bit too baggy now and maybe a bit too green as well. What about her boots? Should she put them inside or outside her jeans? A year ago she would have ignored her daughter. She'd always been confident about the way she dressed. She felt old; maybe it was in contrast with her daughter who seemed to fit perfectly into the world that surrounded them, maybe it was her marriage, Jonathan, their lack of intimacy. She hoped it was just a phase though and that soon she would feel good again, find the right skin to slide into.

The next day, after visiting the Van Gogh museum, sitting at the terrace of a café, Juliette took out her mobile phone, checked her messages. Catherine had found a paper, a large tabloid that had been left behind by a British tourist. It was large enough for her to hide behind it. The waiter came to take their orders; coffee with milk and a diet coke. Mother and daughter smiled at each other and then both looked away.

Words sent back and forth through some mysterious medium kept on popping up or disappearing off the little screen of Juliette's metallic blue phone. Catherine read them through a gap between the pages of her paper.

Good day, yeah.

Van Gogh Museum

Ya know the one who cut off his ear.

Tattoo??? Whatd'ya mean?

Cool, where?

Ask him

Behind her paper, Catherine let her mind wander. The atmosphere of the town was easy, relaxed. The day had been good; she felt younger, freer than she had for a long time, her life white pages waiting to be filled.

When she was last in Amsterdam, she'd been carefree and unknowingly young. She could vaguely remember what she had done but not what she had felt. In that sense the few days were slightly blurry, all merged into one. Fragments of vibrant colours, musty smells and hushed voices were tucked away safely in her memory, but her recollection of emotions had faded into time.

She closed her eyes and lowered the paper, exposing her face to the warmth and brightness of the sun. 'The Woman in Blue', seen the day before at the Rijksmuseum, was standing before her, bathed in light, oblivious to the painter, all her senses directed towards the letter. The light stopped somewhere half way across her face though; there was a shaded patch on her cheek and neck. Catherine's hand let go of the newspaper and thinking of the dark place on the painting, she touched her cheek and neck. Then, her hand moved up to the back of her ear. Her skin, soft, very soft, no flesh, hard bone beneath. Something inside her stirred. She sat up, pulled back her shoulders, pulled in her stomach, tensed her thighs and buttocks, repositioned her feet. That little bit of skin, untouched for years, held memories that she had pushed away. His hands, not very big but strong, had held her face tightly. His thumb had gently rubbed that place behind her ear and then slowly made its way down her neck to her collarbone. She remembered his eyes; a warm colour, yellow almost.

Juliette was looking at her. "Are you all right?"

"Yes, fine darling." Catherine wished to be on her own. She was just beginning to recall the night she had spent with that man-boy – Henkie was his name, or was it? She wanted to make out the outline of his body, remember his smell.

"Mum, I've just been texting Martie."

Another interruption, pulling her away from her memories: her daughter making contact. She let go of the vision of a round shoulder and re-entered the time and the place she was in.

"Ah, how is she?"

"She's, like, very well."

"Good."

"She, she said something, like, about her sister getting a tattoo done when she came here."

"A tattoo? What a strange idea."

"Not that strange really, it's just like having your ears pierced, innit?"

"Not quite." Catherine paused and folded the paper, neatly.

"Well mum, I'd really, really like to get one."

"What?" Catherine looked up. "A tattoo?"

"Yes a tattoo."

"Really? What shape?"

"Not sure yet, maybe a heart. What do you think, mum?"

"I don't know, I'm thinking... Once there, it's there to stay you know... You're young, you might regret it."

"No I won't, I'd really, really like one; it won't be big. Lots of girls at school have one. It will remind me always of this place and of, of this time in my life."

"You will change. You might not want to always be reminded of 'this time' in your life, of being sixteen."

"Why not? I like being my age, I'm, like, having a good time. I won't change that much."

Had she, Catherine, herself changed? Do people ever really change? The teenager she once was, the hopes she had; had all that been erased or just covered year after year by more and more layers of life?

She had never liked tattoos. Some people literally hid their skin behind them, others used them as symbols of creed or never ending love. Slightly ridiculous, was there really such a thing as never ending love? Life happened, it might take your loved one away, bring you another one, and then what do you do, get another tattoo? She guessed that's what they did, with each new phase, a new tattoo, to remember that slice of life with.

"Muuum… what are you thinking about?"

"What your father would say," she lied. "Whereabouts would you like your tattoo?"

"On the hip I think, or the ankle. Or, like, at the base of my back."

"You mean the top of your bottom?"

"Well… Yes, I guess so…. So what do you think?"

"I don't know. It's not a no. For now it's just a question mark. Let me think about it."

When they got back to the hotel, Sjap offered them a coffee and impulsively Catherine accepted. They sat in a terraced area at the back of the hotel, untamed greenery peppered with small white flowers surrounding them. The coffee was good, strong, but softened by hot frothy milk. Juliette had a fizzy, juicy drink, cold. Ice cubes clashing into each other in a tall glass. Sjap leaned for a while on the edge of a chair.

"So you are 'ere for one more day only?"

"Yes, it's been lovely though" said Catherine.

"And what vill you do tomorrow?"

"Not sure yet. Our flight is at two in the afternoon so we don't have much time."

"And do you not vant to go to the Red Light District? Tourists alvays go there normally."

Juliette laughed.

"No I read about it and I don't think I really want to see it."

Sjap turned towards her, it was the first time Juliette spoke to him directly. "It's not that bad, really. But I guess it isn't so necessary."

"And have you heard of the Tattoo Hospital?" asked Juliette

Sjap's eyes opened wider. "I have not used it much myself, only tvice," and he gestured to his forehead and pointed at the little green bean, "but

I 'ave friends who go a lot.. It is a friendly place."
"Friendly?"
"Vell, yes friendly, and no one I know had an infection there."
"Oh good!" Catherine smiled, how reassuring.
"Yes, good and it's just around de corner from 'ere."
Catherine looked at Juliette who was looking at her.
"You mean it's that funny white and purple place two streets away?"
"Exacdly."
On their last morning they were up early. The coffee tasted smoother and richer than usual.
"On the hip mum, that's where I'd like it."
"Fashion might change, Juliette, you'll have to live with it. Are you really, really sure that's what you want?"
"Yes, mum, I'm definite."
"On the hip it is then."
Today they both enjoyed the orange cheese and brown bread.

When they first entered the shop the pristine whiteness that surrounded them was almost blinding, such a sharp contrast with the street. All was clean and a large white almost translucent board dominated the wall. It was pinned with pictures of the employees who called themselves tattoo artists, and details of the kind of tattoos they specialised in. From the photos they did not seem threatening, they had friendly faces and interesting haircuts.

A man came in and discussed with them what they wanted, details of the "operation". It would be painful, but bearable, the design would be unique – in this case a blue and green heart, and Joris, who specialised in small tattoos, would be doing it.

Juliette disappeared behind a door into a tiny white room. Catherine's angst dissolved while she was waiting, she knew her daughter would be all right. There was no one else in the waiting room, the front of house man was busy in the back. The silence felt calm, not oppressive.

Her mind began to wander and she slowly managed to focus it back on Henkie. It had been a hot night, yet she remembered the cool of his hand and how it, he, had awakened nerves she did not think she had. His body had left something in her, something she could finally recollect now, years later. The feeling it left was like ice trickling down her back, surprising and cold, but pleasant. She thought of Jonathan, she contemplated the coming years, spoiling and comfortable yet somehow bland, lacking energy and she feared she might fall asleep again, forget the life that was inside her.

Juliette came out rather pleased with herself, said it hurt a bit but not that much. She was happy and straight away beep-beep-beeped Martie. Outside the shop Catherine told Juliette to go back to the hotel, she needed to buy some lens solution and would only be a minute.

Tram, train, flight, the journey back was good too. They had a glass of champagne.
"Let's celebrate! The month of June." said Catherine as they clinked their glasses together. When they landed it was Catherine's phone that beeped.
Back early darlings – am at the airport to collect you.
Jonathan seemed lighthearted, hugging them both warmly. Louis, he said, would not be back for another few days. They left the airport arm in arm, Jonathan in the middle. He was keen to find out more, Juliette was chatty, filling him in on all the details of their trip. As she sat in the passenger's seat, Catherine pushed back her hair and lightly stroked that little place behind her ear, wondering if Jonathan would ever find the moon crescent that had been tattooed there.

July | India
Jennie Walmsley

The insistent thrumming of rain on the roof woke Frances, dragging her from the silent depths of sleep. Opening her eyes, she couldn't place herself. The room was dark except for a tiny finger of light around the curtain. She checked the clock – 4.40 already. She didn't know how long she'd slept, she felt as if she was still on the plane, neither at home, nor landed.

She padded across the room, pulled back the curtain and opened the French windows. A wave of warm air rushed in – jasmine, traces of garlic and turmeric frying, and the earthy scent of wet mud. Raindrops skittered off the table and chairs, splashing onto her bare feet.

Leaving the doors open, she went to the bathroom and showered. Drying off, she caught sight of her reflection. She was still slim. Good genes and pilates, oh, and a year of grief. Grief had its uses, she smiled grimly to herself. At least she'd avoided joining the other village women at Weight Watchers, carefully totting up the calories in their vodkas and tonics. Pete would have got the joke. He had always appreciated her self-deprecating humour, the way she laughed at the smallness of her female life, and the parochial concerns of her contemporaries – worries about inappropriate planning applications, whether people were cleaning up their dog shit. Somewhere along the way they had become stereotypes, supportive wives and mothers, cooking endless bolognaise, supervising tedious hours of homework, ensuring university applications were sent, bills paid, dinner parties organised. Somewhere along the way, they'd submerged themselves in the lives of others. Pete's death, at least, had released her from that.

Black linen trousers, a white shirt, and moisturiser smoothed onto her face. Frances examined her eyes in the mirror, peering into their brown depths. There were crows' feet now, and soft shadows. She recognised that the smile she practised fell short of her eyes. Her phone beeped – a text message from Andrew: B thr 5.30. X. She swept a brush through her hair, squirted herself with perfume, brushed her teeth and gargled. That was it. This is how he would find her, nearly thirty years older, 'same, same, but different'.

"Amazing, Fran!"

She didn't know whether his words were a comment on the way she looked, or the hotel, or the fact that here they were meeting again after so long. But he stood there with his arms open like a great comforting bear and she threw herself into them. They stood in the lobby, wrapped silently around one another. He smelt of cotton and incense.

"My God, you're wearing the same perfume. So, let's see how you look," he took her by the elbows, stepping her backwards so that he could examine her face. "Yup, I'd recognise you anywhere. The same."

"Older"

"Yeah, me too. Funny how it doesn't show though, apart from this, in my case," he patted his stomach. "Packed in most of my vices, but the sweet tooth still gets the better of me. Let's go and have a drink, there's a bar through the back here."

He was taking command. Frances felt grateful, and suddenly utterly exhausted. She had made it here, survived the last twelve months, the funeral, the logistics and the howling-alone-nights beneath the duvet, supporting the kids, booking her flights and arranging the hotel. Now Andrew could take up the challenge, guide her to the bar, choose a table, order the drinks.

The downpour had stopped though heavy drips still plonked off the roof onto the floor providing a gentle timpani, accompanied by the pulse of evening cicada. The waiter arrived with their drinks.

"So, where to begin? Good flight? The last three decades?" Andrew smiled.

"Yes, thanks, flight fine. Slight delay in Mumbai. Last three decades, bit of a bumpy ride. Still reeling from the recent turbulence."

"Yes, I'm sure," he paused, "I'm sorry Fran. I can't imagine what's in your head at the moment."

He waited.

She took a gulp from her glass, the bitterness of the gin dissolving on her tongue.

"I don't know either. It all happened so fast. We'd just got back from holiday, packed Megan and Rob up for university. It was going to be us alone again and we were looking forward to it. And then suddenly, 'poof' gone."

She felt the purpling air throbbing with insects, as if the evening was alive.

"He'd gone downstairs to make me some tea. I fell back asleep. When I went down he was on the kitchen floor."

He'd been lying face-down, and when she'd lifted him there'd been blood smeared over the tiles where his face had landed. That's how they'd known he'd died instantly. He hadn't put his hands out to break his fall. He was dead before he hit the ground. That's what they'd said. She didn't know if it had been to make her feel better. His eyes had been closed, his nose twisted violently to one side, covered in blood. She hadn't been able to shake the image.

Andrew fished an envelope out of his pocket and handed it to her.

"I found these before I came. I showed them to the boys at the home. They couldn't believe how young I was."

Frances opened the envelope, extracting some photos.

"Look at that fine figure of a man," Andrew continued, "and that beauty there."

He tapped the top photo in her hand. Thirty years dissolved. Two university students, their hair unkempt, beaming smiles, dusty tans. They were in the desert in Rajasthan. She remembered how they'd travelled there by night-train with no air-conditioning, racketing around in bunks with no suspension. They'd spent two nights in the desert with a motley crew of other backpackers and a couple of local guides. They'd shared a camp-bed, cuddling up to one another for warmth as the temperature dropped. They'd had sex for the first time the following night in the grubby hostel. He hadn't been her first lover, but he had been the first one she'd loved.

She flipped over another photo – a close-up of herself, her face covered in sand, chocolate eyes staring from the past into her own.

"Do you remember this?" she asked.

"I think so, wasn't that in Kerala?"

"Yes, on the beach, after a long night of partying."

There had been a lot of long nights of partying during their trip. She recalled barbecues on beaches, bhang lassis that tasted like grass yoghurt and which sent them spinning, too much beer, pirated videos of Elvis in concert, Bob Marley endlessly wailing away on tinny sound systems.

The girl in the photo was wearing a black swimming costume, her hair straggling in rats' tails over sunburnt shoulders.

"You took this picture after you'd saved me."

Andrew looked at her quizzically.

"You know, when I nearly drowned."

She'd been out swimming. It was very late, or very early. The stars had begun to dissolve, and the sky was emptying to a vast black sheet. The sea was warm and equally black. She'd drunk too much. She'd swallowed some water, choking on the salt. Spluttering, she turned onto her back and closed her eyes, floating with her arms outstretched like a giant starfish, the swell of the waves supporting her with gentle rolls. It was like being returned to the womb, surrounded by black amniotic fluid. She lost her orientation, her limbs felt heavy, and she wanted to sleep. It had felt easier to drift than swim, aware only of her body gently being rocked and the silence broken only by her own rhythmic breathing. Then gently, along with the lapping of the water, she'd become aware of another sound. Her name being called, "Fran! Fran!" the sound pulled her back to consciousness. Andrew's frantic voice shouting at her. She raised herself to tread water, and saw his pale staggering figure on the beach, waving at her, calling her. She submerged her head under the surface and began to swim back to shore.

He'd run in at the water's edge and grabbed her. They'd stumbled up the beach and landed on the sand in a heap. He'd stretched his hand out to her and stroked her back. She'd lain there with the light rising on the horizon, resurrected.

There was another photograph of the two of them, taken on their last day travelling together. Here at the railway station, in Madras, as it was then. Both of them were thinner than they'd been in the other pictures.

Frances noticed the pronunciation of her collarbone peeking out from beneath a pale blue open-necked shirt. Andrew's arm was slung around her shoulder, appearing simultaneously to be holding her to his side and steadying her aside. They were standing on a platform, the train's doors open behind them. Her rucksack was on the ground, and she had a plastic bag in her hands, probably containing fruit and water for her journey. Although they were older in this photograph, there was something that looked more vulnerable about them, perhaps because of the weight loss, as if they were pared back almost to their skeletons. Andrew had caught dysentery and spent most of the previous fortnight communing with the hostel's toilets. He hadn't been taking his antibiotics well, too stoned half the time to remember to swallow the horse pills that had been prescribed. The weight had dropped off Frances too, maybe through the worry of caring for him, ensuring he drank enough water, didn't smoke too much. In the picture, both of them were smiling, but Frances' eyes were concealed behind sunglasses. Now, regarding her younger self, she knew she'd been crying, that his decision to stay, not to go back to England to finish his final year, had been a huge burden for her. He had wanted her to stay, but she knew she couldn't. She needed to finish university and she knew she wouldn't be able to save him from himself. He had needed to remain here in the heat and the chaos, slowly descending into his own inferno.

"Do you ever regret not going back with me?" she asked, looking up from the picture of the grinning young man to the older incarnation across the table.

"No. I couldn't. What for? I was nowhere, I was lost, and going back wasn't going to help me find myself. I needed time to clear my head, and university wasn't going to help that. I mean, of course, there are regrets. I'm sorry I never finished my degree. It would have been cool to have been a Bachelor of Philosophy. But what would I have done with that, anyway? Gone to the City, sell people things? I was sorry for a long time about us, about you. But it seemed to be the right decision for you to go back home."

Frances smiled. How could she contradict him? Things had been fine, she'd graduated, met Pete, made a life. She had been happy. But seeing herself in these pictures, being back here with Andrew, even just the warmth, the way her shirt was now sticking to her back in the evening heat, catapulted her back to being someone else.

They ordered another round of drinks, some dhosas, and as they ate, Andrew told her about the home. There were thirty full-time residents – all boys he'd found at the railway station, scavenging lives amongst the commuters and travellers. Boys who'd been abandoned by their parents, or who had run away to make their fortunes in the big city. Kids without roots, who'd beg or steal, or worse, to survive.

"The first one, Prem, the one who made the difference, is a dad now. He works in a hotel downtown. He tried to nick my camera. It was a couple of months after you left. I'd calmed down quite a lot by then. I'd cleaned up, wasn't smoking any more, but I was still thinking about coming home. I was near a temple just buying myself a drink when I felt this hand going into my bag. I turned around and I grabbed it," as he said this Andrew fist clenched in re-enactment. "The swell of rage was huge. I suppose I'd shifted the drugs out of my system but testosterone's harder to get rid of, and I nearly hit the living daylights out of him. As I swung him around – this thin, wiry dark boy, he was only eleven or so at the time so I nearly lifted him off his feet – I saw his face," Andrew put his outstretched hand up to the right side of his face, dragged it slowly down his cheek, past the small mole she'd forgotten. "All of it was puckered and scarred. It was half melted away. He'd been working at the station, making and selling chai for one of the gangs and a pan of boiling water had been knocked all over him. Nobody had been around to look after him. He didn't have any family. He'd survived it, but alone. If he'd had proper medical care, the scarring wouldn't have been so bad."

Frances watched Andrew. He rested his eyes gently on her.
"That's what really kept me here. Prem and his friends. I just couldn't walk away, suddenly I felt needed. You'll see. Finding a way to help them became an obsession, a purpose. They're lost boys. For them I was a responsible adult. I could help them. It started with me applying a bit of first aid now and then to the kids I met on the streets, and slowly snowballed until I had to set up the home, and adopt some. And then, of course, I met Smita, and we got married, and, and... So here it is, here I

am thirty years later."

They finished their drinks. The waiter brought the bill, Frances batting Andrew's hand away to sign for it.

"On me. You've renounced all this money stuff, whereas I, member of the rat race that I am, have it – plenty. Pete's insurance made sure of that."

They strolled out to the front of the hotel, along the carefully swept path between ornate iron lamps that shed pools of orange light. Out of the darkness, a small figure emerged and moved towards them. Frances instinctively halted, almost stepping backwards from the slight boy in shorts and tatty T-shirt with "Madonna World Tour 2006" emblazoned across his scrawny chest. Andrew caught her hand, and then immediately dropped it again, turning to her,

"Don't worry, that's Sonny, he won't hurt you. He's with me".

Frances exhaled and laughed at the same time,

"Sorry, I didn't realise. What's he doing here? Has he been waiting all this time?"

"Yes, he's got time to wait. Rather wait for me here, than wait somewhere else. Anyway, he's been guarding my bike".

He nodded a little further on, indicating the motorcycle. Even to Frances' untrained eye, it was a beautiful machine, black and gold, polished and shiny. Andrew climbed onto it.

"It's a classic Enfield. See I haven't completely renounced possessions, and it suits me, don't you think?"

She thought there was something reminiscent of Easy Rider about him. Sonny clambered pillion behind him.

"I'll see you at the station in the morning. Eight's early enough."

Andrew's foot lurched the motorcycle into action, and he smiled, "It's good to see you again Fran."

He pulled away, the bike swerving away from the path and onto the main road, its red light a beacon in the night. She stood watching it and him retreat, the slight silhouette of Sonny curled like a diminutive shadow behind his back.

Frances was at Central Station earlier than eight. She had fallen asleep quickly, but had been woken before dawn by the distant sound of peacocks calling to one another. Their harsh cries reached into her dreams and pulled her to the surface. Unable to hunker back into the oblivion of sleep, she'd made some tea and sat at the terrace table watching the bleary colours of dawn arrive over the gardens at the rear of the hotel. She re-examined the photos Andrew had given her, and then placed them safely inside the diary she had brought from England. It was the journal she'd kept when she and Andrew had been travelling, the one she'd found when sorting out papers after Pete's death. It had been stuffed with thin blue airmail letters Andrew had sent her after she'd gone back home. And a few tattered Christmas cards. Then their correspondence had shifted to occasional e-mails, annual round-robins summarising thirty years of separation. But it had been enough to keep contact between them. And he'd e-mailed her when he'd heard about Pete's death: "Come to Chennai. Nothing better than the chaos and tropical heat of this place to blow away the cobwebs." She'd agreed. She wanted to see Andrew again. The night before had reassured her that what she'd remembered was real. He was still funny and open. What she had remembered was right, he was one of her life's constant threads.

She ordered a cab to take her to the station. She sat in the rear of the rackety Ambassador, window rolled down, allowing the milky wind to bathe her with its morning scents. The road was potholed and as the driver swerved to avoid them, Frances was thrown from one side of the bench seat to the other, and had to grab onto the strap to steady herself. There was something amusing about being ricocheted around like this, something playful and unrestrained.

The station was heaving with people when she arrived, some with clear intent to catch a train, or buy a ticket, or disembark and launch into the business of their day in the city. But plenty of the people seemed to be purposeless, to be standing, surrounded by bags and children in the growing heat, absorbing the noise and colour and chaos. Frances joined them, knowing that she wasn't camouflaged, that a middle-aged white woman standing alone in the middle of this human soup was out of place. This had been where she and Andrew parted. She didn't recognise it, except for the teeming humanity. The hall was large and echoey, the sound of trains and doors slamming, the shouts of vendors, whistles blowing, a constant buzz of activity. Frances felt like a silent invisibility in the midst of it all. Although she knew her appearance might attract some attention, she was also aware that she had no clear identity here. She might as well have been a column or a wall. Frances noticed an old woman sitting on the floor like a barnacle, immobile in a sea of scurrying feet and trolleys. The old woman's thin arm outstretched from beneath her tattered white sari in supplication. The tide of Chennai's rush-hour ignored her too.

The station tannoy was announcing an imminent departure for Mumbai when the crowd parted, almost magically, and a small group, led by Andrew walked towards Frances. Sonny was by his side, she recognised him, not so much by his face as by his T-shirt. He held a small garland of jasmine flowers in his hands which he slung around her neck, then stepped back and placed his hands together, slowly raising them to his forehead as he bowed. She namasted in return.

"Morning, Fran," Andrew beamed at her over the heads of a gaggle of stringy children, most of whom hardly came up to his shoulder, "this is just the welcoming party. The rest of the boys are back at the Home cooking up a feast with Smita. But Sonny and co wanted to greet you here, they wanted you to see their home turf."
He swept his arm expansively across the station concourse.
"Sonny used to scavenge down near platform 3. That was before he decided he wanted to be a mechanic," he scruffed his fingers through Sonny's hair. "The Home's about five minutes away, are you happy to walk?" Frances nodded, and found herself surrounded by the gaggle of children, one or two of whom took her arms almost as if to lift her out of the place. They were like little birds, twittering away between themselves, giggling with one another, obviously talking about her. One of the smaller boys whose dark brown face was marked with poxy scars, put his hand in hers. His hand was tiny, the bones fragile, like porcelain.

Andrew's presence seemed to centre the gang of children as they walked. They circled him like satellites, brushing up against him, patting his arm reassuringly, telling him some joke. Sonny was always just a step behind Andrew, gently chiding the smaller ones to keep pace. They turned into a narrow alleyway with small streams of dirty water skirting its edges.

Although shady, the grubby whitewashed walls seemed to close in, suffocating them, the air heavy with the promise of rain. Andrew led them into a paved courtyard, at the far end of which was a breeze block building hidden by drooping fronds of some tropical climber. In front of the verandah, a prominent blue board announced "The Railway Children" in vibrant yellow.

The verandah opened onto a large room with a ceiling fan and low-slung cushioned benches, where some of the children slept at night, Andrew explained. In the day, the room was the general meeting point, a lounge where the kids paid homage to either of the shrines. Andrew indicated one corner dominated by a large TV and DVD and another which boasted a huge picture of Shiva, and various grotesque plaster of paris models of Ganesh, gold tinsel, beads and smouldering incense. "God and Mammon," Andrew smiled.

On the other side of the main corridor was the office, and behind that Andrew and Smita's bedroom and a bathroom. Upstairs were four bedrooms packed ingeniously with bunkbeds. Behind the main block was another larger courtyard with raised vegetable patches. Around its edges were buildings, sheds really, each with freshly painted signs indicating their function – 'Workshop', 'Music room', 'Dorm 1', 'Dorm 2', 'Infirmary', 'Kitchen'. Pans clattered inside the latter, followed shortly after by the appearance of Smita, a small woman in a dark purple sari, bearing a tray of cold drinks. "Welcome, Frances. Come, let's go on the verandah. Let's sit, it's too hot to be dragging around. You can look around more later." Despite the fact that Smita was smaller than many of the boys, they clearly deferred to her, and she seemed to direct them with barely perceptible movements of her head.

For the next half an hour Frances found herself introduced to a series of young boys, some almost men, their upper lips brushed with soft moustaches. Some approached her diffidently, extending their hands in formal handshakes, others bowed. Some brought her bowls of nuts, or ran to refill the jug with cold water at Smita's bidding. Another and another and another. Frances tried to study each one, to remember some distinguishing feature. Each one without a family, each one picked up off the street, dusted down, washed, de-loused, made presentable and presenting themselves to this formal white woman, Andrew's important guest. She registered their eyes flickering over her, lowering their gazes beneath their eyelashes when she caught their eye, gauging her wealth and her worth.

The morning dissolved. Fat raindrops falling onto the courtyard, plopping off the leaves of the plants. Children appearing and disappearing to perform different tasks – sweeping floors and serving food. Andrew explained how they tried to equip them with skills so that they could learn a trade: for some that meant they worked in the office on the computer, learning word processing skills and how to do spreadsheets. Others concentrated on cooking, hoping to get an apprenticeship in one of the city's restaurants. "I'm a member of the local Rotary Club," Andrew stood up prompting Frances to do likewise, "I squeeze every last bit of guilt out of Chennai's great and good. If they won't donate large amounts of cash to run this place, they can donate something useful or offer boys placements in their businesses, so they don't have to steal anymore. These lads need a purpose, a role." Andrew's words fell heavily on Frances. What purpose or role did she play now? Suddenly unencumbered by maternal or matrimonial roles, she was free-floating, anchorless. Despite her feminist principles, it was her relationships with the kids and Pete which had positioned her over the last three decades.

Andrew encouraged her to make herself at home whilst he went off to do some work, "Computerisation hasn't diminished Indians' love of paperwork – now we just have to print everything out several times. Can I leave you while I go and send some e-mails in triplicate? I'm sure Smita could use a hand in the kitchen, we'll eat in an hour or so, when most of the boys who go out to work will be back. Wander round, talk to the kids, join in with whatever they're doing."

Frances joined two boys sitting cross-legged on the verandah floor. They were busy rolling up rope coiled in vast snakes across the wooden floor. She didn't know what the purpose of the task was – the boys didn't speak English, but it was clear from their hand-gestures they were pleased with her methodical work.

When the rain stopped, she left them to finish the last length, and drifted through the house to the kitchen where Smita was busy stirring ingredients in a bowl, her scarf fallen back from her head and draped over her shoulders revealing a long black plait.

"What are you making, can I help?" Frances asked.

"Andrew's favourite pudding, my own recipe. He likes sweet things, but I try to use less fat; I'm trying to help him lose weight." Frances noted the way Smita said this as if she were asserting her role as indulgent, but firm, provider. Smita deftly rolled small patties of the sticky concoction into balls between her palms, placing them in concentric circles in a plate. Frances began to do the same, "What's in them, they smell delicious?"

"Cardoman, almonds, rice flour, rose water, honey. I use honey rather than sugar. Your husband sold honey, no?"

"Yes, Pete was a honey importer. The UK's largest importer actually. Money in honey; pots and pots of the stuff..."

"I'm sorry for your loss. It is hard to lose a husband. My first husband died in a car crash."

"I didn't know you were married before Andrew. Did you have children?"

"No, no children. I was very young," Smita began to spoon the balls of dough into a pan on the stove, "I was very lucky to find Andrew. Most Indian men would not have accepted me. My family were not too pleased. They cannot accept him, but I have a new family now. Plenty of kids." The oil in the pan sizzled as each ball hit the fat.

"But losing one thing made space for something else." She scooped the balls out of the fat, shook them and dropped them in a bowl of ground almonds.

"What will you do now?" she asked, turning the heat off, and glancing at Frances.

"I'm leaving tomorrow to go North, see some sights."

"You are welcome to stay here if you would like."

"Thank you... I'm due to meet Megan in Delhi," Frances put her hand gently on Smita's. "But it's been lovely to meet you and the boys... And to see Andrew again."

"You are welcome," Smita continued to stir her hands vigourously through the ground almonds.

Frances rinsed her hands and indicated she was going to look around the rest of the home.

She walked around the fresh puddles in the courtyard to the music room. It was empty. Andrew had shown it to her, like some precious jewel, "I've just finished soundproofing it," he'd proudly touched the walls which were an exercise in DIY ingenuity – thin foam mattresses tacked to the unpainted walls. "We have to try and protect the neighbours from the racket! The boys come in here at all hours. Most of the equipment, like this piano's been donated. I've just bought the drum-set. Some of the boys have got a band. They like to play rock classics and punish the locals with tortured versions of Stairway to Heaven" He'd smiled, "It's good therapy."

Frances closed the door quietly behind her. The room was hot and stuffy. Small particles of dust eddied in the light from an unsheathed lightbulb hanging by a cord from the ceiling. She sat down on a stool behind the drumset and picked up the drumsticks. She tapped the cymbal experimentally. The sound was pure, definite. She hit it again, then one of the smaller drums, followed by one of the larger. She felt the vibrations through her chest. She hit it again and again. And again. The blinding escalation of the noise encouraged her on. She hit harder and harder, louder, more frantically, as if her life depended on it. Each impact of stick on drumskin pushed her forwards, so that her arms thrashed and flailed. She felt possessed, each beat a statement about her presence, a lash of undirected anger. It was as if she couldn't stop. Her face was wet with sweat and tears, and she could hear herself whimpering beneath the beat.

She stopped. The room filled with silence, except for her own sharp intakes of breath. The door opened behind her, damp heat from outside melting into the suffocation of the shack. Quietly lying the drumsticks down and lifting her sleeve to her face, she wiped away sweat and a slug of snot before turning.

"Hello, Miss Frances. Are you OK in here?" a slight figure silhouetted against the daylight stepped into the room, holding a glass of water out to her. It was Sonny. She took the glass without looking at him, her head lowered; a 'thank-you' in her two-handed acceptance of the glass and the incline of her body towards him. The water was cold.

"Would you care to see the bike? I am fitting new mirrors today. Do you want to see?"

She nodded and followed Sonny from the room down a small covered alleyway to where the Enfield was parked. Next to the bike was a bucket of water.

Sonny touched the bike lovingly, encouraging her to do the same with gentle hand movements. The boy said nothing to indicate he had heard the noise or seen her tears. His interest was in showing her the beauty of the metal, the shine he was polishing onto its chrome. "It's called a Bullet. This is authentic vintage styling. Classic look, but good speed."

She perched herself on a low wall and watched as he passed his leather cloth across the bike's surface, pointing to various bits and fiddling with the new rear-view mirrors. She only half listened as he regaled her with the bike's technical details. She wondered at his age, fourteen, maybe? He gave off that sense of throbbing growth, as if one could almost see the adult body pushing its way through the childish bulb–like form. Sonny's chatter about the bike's capabilities reminded her of the way Rob could recite football statistics at the same age, that almost autistic memory for detail.

She wanted to show him she understood the importance of the bike, "Do you ever ride the Bullet by yourself?" Sonny's face lit up with a wide smile.

"Yes, once or twice, Andrew has taken me out of town and let me ride her alone. Very illegal." She sensed the thrill in his voice.

"But I know how to control her," he continued. "And I like very much riding solo – you feel the wind in your face in a different way, steer the course, take charge. You can't ride pillion forever."

"Why are you here, Sonny?" the question spilled from her mouth before her head had had time to consider it.

Sonny didn't withdraw his hands from their work, the tightening of the mirror screws requiring the concentration of his gaze.

"Andrew brought me here two years ago. I escaped from bad men. I stole for them at the station. From people like you. When I didn't steal enough, they beat me."

He glanced at her, his words sitting quietly between. She didn't know what to say, there was something confessional in what he said, although he did not appear to be asking for any particular response.

"What do you think of Andrew?" she asked.

"He's a good man. Andrew looks after us, keep me safe. It's normal, it feels like family. The other boys are like brothers. I like to look after the bike. Next year will start as an apprentice at the Enfield factory. I love motorcycles."

He described his position with such simplicity. It was matter of fact, lacking in self-pity, said with certainty.

"What about you?" Frances was surprised by his confidence in throwing a question back at her, though she was uncertain whether he was asking her reason for being there or her view of Andrew.

"Andrew is an old friend. I have had a hard time recently and it seemed a good time to catch up with him. Andrew and I travelled together here a long time ago, when I was a little older than you."

"Did you travel by bike?" The boy shifted the conversation back to his territory.

She nodded, "We did for some of our trip, not all. It was something like this one, though less shiny. Less well cared for." Sonny smiled at the compliment, polishing the mirrors with a chamois leather, "And you know, I always seemed to ride pillion."

"Andrew loves the Bullet. But it takes a lot of care, and the roads here are not good. She needs lots of cleaning, especially at this time of year. Lots of mud. Lots of potholes always jumping out at you unannounced, and bad drivers. Last night coming back from your hotel, someone knocked this mirror, that is why I am replacing it."

"Yes," she said, "I know how those potholes jump out at you. You get buffeted around, thrown off course. And it's important to have mirrors – see what's behind you."

A bell rang. "That's dinner," Sonny tucked his chamois into his shorts and held out his hand to help Frances up from the wall.

"Sonny, after dinner can I go out on the bike?"

He nodded and a smile seeped across his face. Frances smiled back.

August | Barcelona
Rachel Jackson

Everything was so unfeasibly shiny. Even the pavement seemed to shimmer and melt beneath her as she stepped hesitantly along it. Las Ramblas was shockingly busy and bright, too bright for Isla, who felt dangerously exposed even in her sunhat and factor thirty cream. The famous boulevard seemed to swim slightly, giving the impression that the chattering crowds, the buskers and the glinting shop fronts were all under water. As she squinted into the haze, the wheel of her weekend case caught on a paving slab and she stumbled. Perhaps the two G&Ts and four mini bottles of red she had downed on the plane had been a mistake, though God knows how else she would have got through her ordeal. It had been one of those bargain flight jobs, worryingly cheap, and she always fretted that the savings had been made by skimping as blithely on safety as they did on comfort. How absurd she was to worry when it was quite clear to her that everything was completely out of her hands.

The warm alcoholic fug that had settled inside her so comfortingly during the flight now made her feel queasy, unwholesome and foolish. Isla avoided drinking on normal days, just like her parents, ever since Uncle Jonjon had dropped dead of some unmentionable liver disease within three years of retiring from the army. Still, fortification had been required as soon as she'd reached Stanstead, although she now saw that it didn't mix well with the Barcelona heat, which surely had to be hitting thirty today. She swayed onwards, wondering whether she might simply dissolve or turn violently crimson in the sweltering sunshine. The eternal curse of the redhead.

Isla kept casting up nervous glances at anything that vaguely resembled a café, whilst trying to keep her eyes off the nut-brown legs of the local girls who sauntered along, shrieking and gesturing. Some carried towels, other had bikini halter-necks peeping from under their T-shirts. There was a beach around here somewhere, so she'd read online without much interest. In less than an hour, she had decided that the endless parades of shops and the showy architecture spoke of a city that had plenty of everything already, even without the greedy serendipity of being placed right next to the sea. Barcelona promised to be a bit too much.

It was now 12.04 pm, she was officially late. She might have already passed No.175, but hadn't seen any numbers at all yet. Together with a friend she might have found it by now, but at that moment, alone, she felt strangely ineffectual. Maybe a solo trip had not been such a brilliant idea, but with only one place left on the weekend it was either that or forfeit the holiday. Besides, holidaying alone was precisely the sort of thing one ought to have done before turning twenty-five and she only had one month left to go.

She faltered on for a few steps, then turned around and started to walk back the way she had come. Perplexed, she turned again and walked on. There, not ten yards ahead, was the Boqueria market and the right café, just next door. She reached into her cavernous bag for a tissue, dabbed her brow and cheeks and tried to prepare herself, though for what she was not too sure. Just people, all tourists, like her. It would be fine.

Pushing through the café door, she sighed aloud at the blast of air-conditioning on her pink face. The group were not hard to spot. Twenty or so people had taken over a few tables in the corner and two of them, a man and a woman in their thirties, were wearing the turquoise holiday rep polo shirts. The woman was addressing the group in strongly accented English. Isla gave a tight, embarrassed little smile to no one in particular and sidled into the nearest chair.
"... so that means you can learn at least three hours of salsa each day. We will give you the itinerary, but you can join each item or not as you please..."

Isla, feeling her blood cool and settle, furtively tried to assess her fellow dancers. Four couples, all middle-aged, including a brassy woman who kept digging her husband in the ribs with excited little nudges. A man in his sixties looking moustachey and earnest. Four well-groomed women in their forties standing together, clearly friends. Two girls a few years younger than her, sipping bottled beers with lemon stoppers. Another woman lingering at the back, sixty-odd, a bit Sunday school teacher. That was it. These were to be her companions on her one, lost weekend.

Just then another man walked into the cafe, young and unmistakably English, scraping a chair out of the way to get to the group. He dressed like an art student: scuffed up black jeans, red T-shirt with black graffiti all over it.
"Sorry I'm late," he beamed at everyone and then sat down next to Isla.

Isla looked away and wondered when she'd get to look at the itinerary. She could feel that slight, sobering-up headache, as if the sun had leeched all the alcohol out of her pores on her short walk down Las Ramblas. She just needed to get her throbbing head around exactly what was expected of her. That way she could plan a little, be prepared, maybe even get ahead. That way she was far less likely to make a fool of herself.

So this was Diego's Dance Studio. Altogether more promising than the slightly comical name had suggested. Mirrors stretched from the wooden floor to the high ceiling and the air was icy fresh. The chestnut-skinned chest-on-legs chatting to the rep in the corner was presumably the eponymous Spaniard himself. Members of the group sauntered in, in hushed, bright-eyed clusters, all looking straight over at Diego and his tight, white T-shirt. Isla stood apart, her stomach tensing. Perhaps she should have had a go at this back home first, just a couple of classes. Her doubts increased as she took in the schoolteacher woman, still looking matronly despite a scarlet gypsy top and floral skirt. She had spotted Isla and was approaching her, beaming.
"Gosh, I do hope this is alright," she breathed. "Ever done it before?"
"No, never," Isla replied, leaning back a bit.
"I'm Joan, by the way. D'you reckon that's him?" she eyed Diego like a red kite spotting a dead rabbit.
"I presume so," Isla concurred.
"You'll have to help me keep up, you youngsters are better at this sort of thing."

Happily, just then it started. A bright, sensual, salsa tune, pouring knowingly into the gaps between the awkward conversations around the room. Diego sauntered up to the centre, arms held aloft.

"Now. We are all here?"

People looked at each other, clearly unsure. The female rep came up waving a clipboard and a sheet of stickers.

"Everyone take one, with your names, please."

They politely queued up to peel off the labels until just one remained.

"Stephen? Is Stephen here?"

A glance around confirmed he was not. Had to be the same man who was late yesterday. One of those, thought Isla, crossing her arms over her chest. In the chilly room, her top now felt too flimsy and for a moment she thought of cooler climes, of London and the time that must come after this weekend, but quickly tried to shake it from her mind.

Diego clapped his hands and ordered that they line up in two rows facing him. Isla took her place in the second one, but not next to Joan.

"First, the basic salsa step..."

All watched him attentively, Isla concentrating especially hard. He stepped, they repeated; he turned, they copied. Isla stepped along, not swinging her hips too conspicuously, trying to get a feel for the rhythm. Just as she was getting into it the door flew open.

"Sorry, sorry..."

Stephen jogged over to the group and took his place at the end of the first line. He turned and gave a quick grin to those behind him. Isla continued to stare at Diego's preposterous chest.

The class warmed up quickly, with their teacher accelerating the pace at which he relayed new steps, clapping hard to accentuate the sultry rhythm. There was much laughter and exclamation as the beginners lost their footing or turned the wrong way, but Isla didn't join in. She was determined not to get it wrong; it was important to show she was listening.

At the end of the first hour they had learned a simple sequence of steps. Isla felt the tug of anxiety growing as the time went on. They'd been told they would partner up but there were too few men. If she was lucky she'd either get the old guy, or this Stephen bloke, and he didn't seem to be taking it too seriously at all. Not ideal, either way.

Diego clapped again and strode back to turn off the music.

"Is time for partners. Salsa is moving together, responding with lover."

There were a few more giggles which Isla ignored.

"Now, ladies," smiled Diego. "I have very good surprise for you."

He walked over to the main door and opened it. In walked six men, dressed in white T-shirts and black trousers, as dark as Diego and similarly built, though ranging in ages from late twenties to fifty. Isla bridled at the coarse ripple of excitement that ran through the female element in the room.

"This," he waved at them proudly. "Is my friends. Excellent dancers, show you how to move like Spanish women. Now, in twos, you, go with him, you..."

Whilst the couples were kept together, Stephen and the older man were paired up with the teenage girls and the four older ladies, Joan and Isla were each waved towards one of the new dancers. Isla felt the knot inside her tighten further as she was led to a stocky man in his thirties.

"Andreas," he pointed at his chest.

"Isla," she replied.

He nodded and she sensed that the conversation was exhausted. Good. She also fancied that she could feel the envious gaze of the wives as they prepared to have their toes trampled by their husbands. Good again. Now she could be truly authentic.

"OK. First, the way we stand."

The music started up again and the class were taken through the right way to hold and move with their partner, with Diego and the rep demonstrating, everyone else copying. Isla narrowed her eyes and focussed on her feet, receiving small nods of encouragement from Andreas. It was tricky, but she was doing well, with barely a step out of place.

"And now we are going to try the *Dile Que Non*. It means 'tell him no'..."

The complicated move was demonstrated and everyone tried to fumble out their own versions. Isla felt a smug little thrill as her feet fell into the right place first time. Diego stopped dancing and walked over, right up to her.

"Now you see this lady," Diego placed his hand on her shoulder. Isla was suddenly aware of the sweat shining across her forehead. "She has good rhythm."

She bit her bottom lip with pleasure.

"However. She is doing what all you English ladies do. This."

He launched into a horrid little sketch of a baby elephant frowning and stamping its way through the right steps. A hot burst of mortification exploded across her cheeks.

"Is not right. You do not step the steps. You follow your partner," he stabbed a finger towards Andreas, "he leads, you follow. OK?"

Isla nodded rapidly, longing for everyone to look away from her.

"Women! Is not England. Follow your man. All close eyes, now."

Isla quickly snapped her eyes shut and awaited instruction. She could feel the hairs on Andreas's arms brush against her as he pulled her into the hold. It now felt absurdly intimate. Before she could stop herself she felt her body arching away from him, so her chest didn't press too firmly into his.

"OK?" he asked quietly.

Isla nodded, just wanting to get on with it. Andreas rocked forward and she immediately stepped on something yielding.

"God, sorry," her eyes flew open.

"No problem," came the reply. "Eyes. Follow."

Isla closed her eyes again and held her breath. He rocked her and this time her foot moved back. Then a light pressure in the small of her back, brought her forward. And again, and again.

"See?"

Isla, gave a small smile into the darkness. It was an extraordinary sensation being completely led, and, once you got used to it, not entirely unpleasant.

"Good," Andreas encouraged. "Turn."

She stepped awkwardly, but they managed to change direction. They rocked in the basic step a bit longer, then with her eyes still closed, they tried it again. It was better.

"Good. You follow."

"I follow," agreed Isla, feeling some of the tension ease from her shoulders.

"Eyes open. Follow," Andreas commanded.

Isla made herself look at Andreas. He had a raised mole just above his left cheek which she fixed her gaze on, rather than stare straight into the cloudy eyes. They carried on through several changes of music, and even she could feel it was entirely different from her diligent stepping of before. Now it felt like something much freer, something lighter, both unknown and familiar.

"OK., thank you everybody," shouted Diego as the music ended. "We are over for today. Clap yourselves."

The group stepped away from their partners and started to applaud, their three hours up. Isla looked around the class and took in the flushed faces; the older man, Bernard, bowing to kiss his partner's hand, Stephen saying something to make his girl giggle, one pink-cheeked married couple not seeming to want to meet each other's eye. Everyone looked slightly different, somehow more real and vulnerable than before.

"Thank you," she said to Andreas and picked up her bag, hat and bottle of water, hoping to hold on to this strange lightness as she made her way to her hotel. She was the first one out of the studio. As she stepped into the afternoon sun, just for a second, before she remembered not to, she tipped her head right back and let the golden heat warm her face.

Having slept well and woken reluctantly, Isla showered and made her way down to the breakfast room on Saturday morning. Sure enough, her group were mostly there already, colonising a row of tables adorned with fussy cloths.

"Hi all," she offered.

"Grab a seat," bossed one of the women. "Just been discussing our plan of attack for Barcelona."

Isla meekly took a chair but no sooner had she sat down than the two teenage girls stood up. Both were wearing threadbare denim shorts and had their hair held back by expensive sunglasses. Off to tan. One couple followed them, also keen to hit the beach. The forty-something friends left next, trailing behind them an invitation to shop, which Joan gleefully accepted. Isla was left with the pair of remaining couples, plus Bernard and Stephen. She suddenly felt a hollow ache and rose to get a roll and some coffee. Her own fault. Why couldn't she be more at ease with them all, at nearly twenty-five?

She sensed someone come up behind her at the coffee machine.

"It tastes like crap but I need the caffeine," remarked Stephen grabbing a cup from the stack. "You enjoying this salsa lark?"

"Yes, it's fun," she replied. "Harder than I thought it would be, but easier too, if you know what I mean."

She felt the heat flood her cheeks. Idiotic.

"Yeah, you're right," said Stephen easily. "I'm Stephen, by the way."

"I know," blurted Isla. "I mean, I remember your sticker. I'm Isla, sorry."

"For what, being Isla?" Stephen laughed.

She opened her mouth to correct him, then realised and gave a small laugh herself.

They walked back with their coffee. Stephen stopped short of the group table and plonked himself down into a seat at a smaller one. Isla hesitated.

"Have a seat," he insisted kicking out a chair with his foot.

She did, worrying that they must seem rude to Bernard and the others.

"I'm off on the Gaudi Trail today. Want to come with me?"

"I can't," she replied.

"Oh right," he yawned extravagantly, stretching confident arms. "Where you off to?"

Isla lowered her eyes and tried to conjure an excuse. Nothing came, bar death or the airport.

"Not sure really, just wandering."

"Well, why not wander with me, then? Only doing the Gaudi thing and some tapas. Yeah?"

"Oh. Alright then," she replied and bit delicately into her roll, which was a bit stale.

Half an hour later she was at Park Guell, vainly trying to immerse herself in the wonder that was the Gaudi Museum. As Stephen strode enthusiastically about the place, exclaiming over this curving chair and that skew-whiff table, she began to regret her decision. It was too hot and he was walking too fast. Moreover all the asymmetric shapes and ghosts of dead geniuses made her feel a bit nauseous, but she didn't dare confess it, nor the fact that she herself had an art degree. After an age, Stephen checked his watch with a flourish.

"We've got to get a move on if we're going to finish before two," he announced.

"OK. Where next?"

"La Sagrada Familia, the cathedral, you know it?"

"Yes, heard about it but never been."

"Good, me neither. Let's grab a quick bite and then go right to the top of the towers."

Stephen turned and walked smartly off and they emerged into the sunshine. They settled in a small bar a hundred yards away, where she subtly edged them towards a spot under an umbrella and he ordered a selection of tapas for two. The queasiness that Isla felt was growing stronger. When the tiny dishes arrived, she tried to enjoy the baby squid in batter, the fiery patatas bravas, the even more fiery chipirones fritos – those perfectly charred and blistered little chillies – the ham croquettes, milky manchego cheese and rich chorizo, but she ate little. Even the chilled glass of sherry Stephen had ordered, without asking, did not put out the small fire in her stomach. He wanted to climb the towers.

Stephen chatted on, oblivious, telling her, or rather boasting, of his travels over the past two years, through Russia, Chile, Cuba and Hong Kong. He already had an undergraduate degree in Spanish, but now wanted to be an architect and this was a sort of final fling for him, before he set about becoming bigger than Gaudi. He would drink in everything here, then digest it all on his four-day trip back as he drove home to London through France. Sounded perfect, didn't it?

Isla had barely absorbed a word, she was so busy chewing on her squid and trying to plan an exit strategy that wouldn't seem ungrateful. Stephen didn't seem to notice, as he enthused about the food, the dryness of real Spanish sherry, the great music, the fantastic, skin-broiling weather. He was so relaxed and effusive, she wondered if he might be gay. Not that it mattered.

"...it's so bloody, I dunno, sexy. Hey, I was practising my *Dile Que Non* in my room last night, were you?"

"No," she lied.

"Come on!"

He leapt up, still chewing and held his arms out in position. A couple of

THE CONTEMPORARY WOMEN WRITERS' CLUB

elderly diners looked up, their watery eyes inscrutable.

"Let's have a quick go."

Isla shook her head and held on to her sherry. Stephen leant over and pulled on her hand.

"Come on, let's get in a bit of practice while we can. Follow."

Isla, half on her feet, saw that resistance would prolong the shame and thought it wiser to humour him. She let him take hold of her, waited for her cue and duly followed. It didn't feel as effortless as it had the day before with Andreas.

"See? We're bloody brilliant. *Dile Que No!*" he yelled, and took her through the intricate step.

They almost did it, but at the last minute she caught the edge of a chair behind her, which scraped loudly. The elderly couple smiled and clapped, whilst Isla backed crossly away.

"Come on," she muttered. "We'd better go if we're going to see this place."

"Sure. Let's roll."

Stephen grabbed the last piece of cheese from the table and ate it where he stood. Then he reached into his pocket and slapped twenty Euros on the table, before Isla could find her purse.

"This way," he ordered and started walking off again.

They clipped through the streets, Stephen striding as ever ahead. Isla was amazed that, on what was his first trip to the city, he seemed to know the way.

"How do you know where we're going?" she puffed, trotting a little to keep up.

"Easy," he replied, flashing her a smile like melted sunshine. "Just look up. Whenever you're in a new city, always look up."

She turned her face skywards and saw what he meant. Dwarfing the skyline before them were the towers of Gaudi's unfinished masterpiece, La Sagrada Familia. The same towers he wanted to climb. Isla started to rehearse excuses in her head, but all of them sounded like lies, except the actual truth. She silently persevered, but nothing else came and soon they were there at the foot of the iconic cathedral.

"Bugger me," gasped Stephen. "It's just... bloody... magnificent. Check this out."

And he was off again, this time to examine the doorways. Isla choked back a sigh and decided it was time. She padded up behind him.

"Listen, Stephen, I'm going to get back. I don't want to be tired for our class."

"What? You're joking!" he exclaimed waving at the church. "This is the best thing in the whole of Spain! This is what it's all about, Isla. This way, follow me."

Isla hesitated, then fought down a pang of failure as she backed away.

"I'm sorry," she muttered. "I'll see you at the class. Thanks very much for lunch."

She quickly dipped into a group of German tourists and waved without turning. Truly impolite, awful. But she had to go, before they got to the bit about whether to take the lift or walk the four hundred steps skywards. How do you tell a man like that that you're afraid of heights? How do you manage, in fact to say anything really interesting about yourself when he's danced with Cossacks and downed mojitos in Havana? He wouldn't want to hear that you dread climbing beyond the first floor, including balconies and ladders, or are terrified of flying, or of having a car, train or bus crash, or scared of spiders, bees, wild roaming dogs of vicious breeds, of getting lost, of having an adverse reaction to illegal drugs, of childbirth, clowns and motorbikes. And he certainly would not want to hear that she had good reason to be afraid.

It would, perhaps, have been easier to explain to him if he hadn't paid for lunch. Everything scared her, including getting burnt by the rays of this incessant heat that was beating down upon her pale scalp. Why she was outside at high noon without a hat she did not know, but no doubt she would regret it. She rushed off, in what she hoped was a southerly direction, pausing only to dig around for the map issued by the reps. On a whim, she turned around to give Stephen a proper wave. Too late, only the laughing German tourists remained. Something twisted inside her that felt like regret, although it could have been the chipirones fritos.

She woke up with a start and reached for her watch. 7.19 am, the last full day already. Yesterday's dance class had been a success. Throughout the group steps were taken more firmly and arms flung wider, whilst Diego had clapped more and shouted less, which was something. Stephen had got there before her, somehow, and nodded a hello, then had seemed to concentrate all his efforts on making his young partner laugh and spin, while she had quietly tried to follow Andreas.

There would be another class at the same time today, after which they'd break for an early supper and meet up again to dance at the Buenavista Nightclub that evening. Almost six hours to kill. She absent-mindedly ran her hand over her breast as she thought where she might go. She knew, of course. It was calling her, as it had for most of the previous evening when she'd wandered alone through Las Ramblas. It could only be La Sagrada Familia, which, she now saw, had astounded her with its Gaudi, perhaps gaudy, architectural flourishes. The towers were the whole point, Stephen had said. If she could just go now, quietly, with no pressure, then she could explain her silly fears to him whilst bathed in triumph, having climbed every last step. It was a plan.
She hurriedly showered and dressed and went down to grab a few bites from the lacklustre breakfast buffet. No one from her group was eating yet another advantage of having risen so early. She gulped down a coffee then rushed outside to bag a taxi.

Twenty minutes later she was there, inside the great building, looking up. The air was filled with a muted chatter, which bubbled with that sound of excited humility you only hear inside great churches. Isla just looked up at the enormous branching columns, which, she could see now, were meant to bring to mind trees. For a moment she wished Stephen were there to explain the big ideas, but no matter, she wasn't here to chat, she was here to climb. Very, very high.

She followed the sign towards the stairs that would lead her nearer to the Nativity Façade and the Passion Façade. Four hundred steps, she'd read. She looked at her flimsy flip-flops. Was it a good idea? Maybe taking the lift would be less daunting, but climbing was the thing. She would have to take the steps, in order to be able to really make an ascent.
Isla started off well, ten then twenty nice, firm, solid steps and none taking her higher than the level of a bedroom landing. Just fine. She let

Some impatient Chinese tourists overtake from behind her. Fair enough, she was slow, but she was simply... acclimatising. Thirty winding steps higher she went. She tried not to think about the flimsiness of the railing beside her or the incompleteness of the building. All perfectly safe. Then she looked down and saw she was already higher than a house: hubris, utter insanity, to look down on churchgoers like God. She froze and let some more tourists overtake her. Her heart was choking its way into her throat, she could feel the old asthma staring low in her lungs. Dizziness was clutching its hand around her chest as she struggled to breath and closed her eyes, seeing only dancing white lights. She had to get down. She put a foot forward to balance herself and it landed on the higher step in front. She paused to catch her breath, eyes still shut and, liking the sensation, simply did it again, going up, not down. And again, four more times, eyes all the time closed. A soothing thought came to her as she climbed, slowly and higher. Anyone who passed her might presume she was blind, not insane or petrified, and leave her alone if she just did this. All she needed to do was put one foot in front of the other. She just had to follow.

So she did, for over two-hundred steps, not counting, just following. Strangely, after a few minutes she felt able, eager even, to open her eyes, as if she should take in her achievement. And, of course, Gaudi's. She slowly opened her eyes a crack and found she could spy the top of the staircase. On an instinct she started to run, before she could change her mind, before she could look down. After a breathless while she had reached the top and, dizziness gone – too late for nausea, she surveyed the view in the Passion Façade. It was a stunning swirl of stone and sky, reaching far higher than man should be able to reach, undeniably exceeding grasp. Isla looked around at the skyline as if she had just come into life, here, several houses higher than the rest of Barcelona. Another thought soothed her, as she snatched back her breath and marvelled at the way she had climbed blindly through God's very own casa.

She really might not die.

The elation remained with her all the way back to the foot of the steps, which she trotted down with ease. It stayed with her through the journey to the dance studios and through her last ever session with gentle Andreas. She danced well, though not perfectly, occasionally missing her footing as she glanced over to Stephen, wondering if he too could see the change in her. When the class ended, with much whooping and applause for Diego, Isla felt somehow ready, primed to explain to Stephen the essence of her change. But he was chatting to the girl he had been partnered with, laughing over something she could not detect from where she stood. It could wait until later. She would parcel up the feeling inside her until they got to the Buenavista that night where they would all dance with the locals. She thanked Andreas and Diego, then quietly slipped away.

Four hours later, Isla waited in reception with several others to get the two minibus taxis to the club. Everyone was in their party best, the older ones particularly seeming to have gone to some trouble. Isla wore a simple dress, white and strappy with a full, knee-length skirt. It was one of her favourites; a dress that whispered, didn't shout.

When it was nearing the time to go, she watched to see if Stephen would emerge from one of the lifts. Finally, just as she was shrugging a wrap around her to go, she saw him hurrying down the main stairs into the lobby. She tried to hang back to talk to him, but Joan was already there, ushering her onto the first minibus. She got on board and watched as he jumped up into the second vehicle. It would have to wait a bit longer.

Minutes later they poured into the club. The music was playing loudly and while it seemed normal to Isla, some of the older people made lame jokes about going deaf, clearly delighted to be transported back to a youth they had surely never enjoyed. Isla felt the need to walk ahead and, muttering something about finding a loo, separated herself from the rest of the herd.

She walked through dancing crowds and stepped onto a dais, looking over everyone's heads, watching couples express years of passion and familiarity with their intimate and surprising moves. Stephen walked over to her, excusing himself through the crowd as he went.
"No chairs here!" he yelled above the music. "Fancy a quick *Dile Que No?*"

Isla nodded and stepped down to the dancefloor. Stephen held her and they executed their learned steps, somewhat stiffly at first, then with increasing confidence. Isla felt the urge to tell him build in her. He needed to understand what she could do. The music changed and they carried on dancing to a slower number until she could bear it no more.

"I climbed it!" she shouted. "I'm sorry about yesterday, I was terrified but I've climbed it."

"What?" replied Stephen.

"La Sagrada Familia. Too scared to do it with you, but I went back and I did it. Sorry."

Stephen twirled her and then replied, smiling. "Well, well done you. I wondered why you'd just buggered off."

"Sorry," repeated Isla and they danced some more.

When the music changed once again, Isla simply stopped moving her feet, prompting Stephen to lead her away from the jumping, swaying dancefloor. He ducked them through some heavy velvet drapes and they found themselves on a balcony, overlooking the neglected garden.

"Thank you for taking me with you yesterday," garbled Isla. "I know I left, but I was really..."

The 'scared' was muffled as Stephen brought his hands to her cheeks and gently pressed at her with his lips. Isla instinctively brought her hand to her chest, then forced herself to relax and lowered it slowly. Quite quickly, his initial tenderness was replaced by something more urgent as he started to kiss her faster, like the way he walked, trying to get something from her that she didn't quite understand. His hands stroked her back, holding her tighter than when they danced, whilst his arms encircled her, feeling too strong and certain to be comfortable, even with her eyes shut. The kiss went on, with Isla trying hard to keep pace, using her mouth at first to slow him, then simply letting it be what it was, falling into it, following his frenetic lead. Her hands fell to her sides and his own continued to explore her, teasing at her stomach over its white sheath, stroking higher and higher, slowing gradually, until it reached the boundary of cotton over her left breast and slipped eloquently inside.

"Don't!" she jerked her head away from him.

Stephen pulled back immediately, a fog of desire and confusion clouding his eyes. Isla saw the density of that fog and, unable to break through it with words, did the next best thing. She ran away, back through the curtains, across the seething dance floor and out into the night.

⁂

"Got to pack," she muttered to herself as she woke.
The thought of the effort required was enough to make her slump back onto her pillows. Another flight, arse. She rolled out of bed in the man-sized T-shirt that served as a nightie and walked over to the mirror. The devastation wreaked by the night before was evident, but not irreparable. Her eyes were red, her face puffy and pale, her eyes smudged with mascara, but it could all be fixed. No permanent damage from the panicked half hour waiting to find a taxi in a dark side street, or the pillow-muffled sobs back in her hotel room.

Isla pulled the T-shirt over her head and looked again. She ran her hand up her throat, just to feel herself swallow, then watched as her hand moved to her left breast, before she could stop herself. There it went straight to it, the lump on the outer side nearest her armpit, the vile little hillock of unwanted tissue that she had been ignoring for nearly three months. She wished it would seep or ache or flare up scarlet red, but it never did. It just lay there, too silent, refusing to disclose its intentions. Her eyes filled with anxious tears as she let her hand, for a moment, become Stephen's. No point dwelling on it now, too late and too shaming, although… it could happen again. Another hand, another time.

She closed her eyes, running her fingers over the swollen skin, trying to remember the lightness. The lightness she had felt at the dance studio had made her feel, somehow, that she probably would not, after all, turn out to be filling up with cancer. The lump would be benign. Benign: a good word, ineffably kind, like the God they had taught her about at primary school. A benign God would not kill her with a disease that spread over her heart. Nor would he let her perish on a rickety old plane, or crash on the way to the airport, or shrivel to nothing in the fierce sun, or keel over from food poisoning after yet another stale breakfast roll.

She really might not die.

She took her hand away and gave a sharp tap on the dressing table. No more. No more fear, no more cancelled appointments. This time, when she got home, she really would go and see someone. It had suddenly all become clear and easy and terribly personal; taken lightly, it suddenly seemed to matter.

Isla rushed her shower, threw her things into her case and carried it down with her to breakfast. There was no sign of Stephen, but the rolls tasted fresher today at least and she'd grown used to the coffee. Check-out was in fifteen minutes and she hurried on through to reception where all the group were waiting with cases. Stephen stood apart chatting at the reception desk. An urge to explain herself welled up inside her. Why did she always feel this need to reason and apologise and justify, with a man she barely knew? Then a thought started to lead her.

She waited until he was taking his receipt, with clumsy words ready in her mouth. She waited. Stephen had snatched up his rucksack and was weaving his way past the numerous cases, muttering goodbyes, saving a flash of a watery smile just for her. Still she waited. The reps had bounced in with clipboards, preparing to count everyone onto the minibuses. Stephen made his way outside heading for his car, and for France. Isla stopped waiting and hurried out into the street, into the already hot sun.

He was by a red Peugeot when she approached.
"Bye then," she called.
He turned without a smile. "Yeah, see ya."
His keys were clinking in his hand and he hunched towards the car door. The silvery light bathed his back and made her want to touch his arms; it was so very bright.
"Sorry I ran off like that," she began.
"It's okay, it's fine, let's forget it," he carelessly replied over his shoulder.
"No, wait. I have a…" The word wouldn't come.
"What?" he muttered, opening the door.
"A, you know, a lump. I have one, just where you were touching me. That's why I ran," she pressed. "I wish I hadn't."
Stephen straightened and fixed her with green-amber eyes.
"Do you mean you're ill?" he asked doubtfully.

"No idea. But I've got to get to a doctor to find out."

Concern mixed with something else, something masked and unreadable rippled across his face.

"Then you'd better go. You'll miss your bus."

"I don't care," she retorted, refusing to drop her gaze despite the harsh sun.

He shook his head and slung his rucksack onto the passenger seat.

"I'm not afraid," she heard herself saying. "I'm coming with you."

His face contorted in frank surprise.

"To bloody Toulouse? You must be joking."

"That's where you're going, isn't it?"

His eyes looked at her properly for the first time that morning and, for a second, he looked almost defiant. Then something broke and gleamed in his gaze and he gave a short laugh.

"But what about the doctor, Isla? Can't see one in France, you've got to get home."

"I know that," she asserted. "But it's only four days. I've waited long enough."

He raked his fingers through his hair then stood, leaning heavily on the bonnet, as if paralysed. Finally, after a moment, he reached inside the car and flung the bag off the passenger seat into the back. He turned back to her, reached over and lightly stroked one finger down her cheek. Then he smiled, just like that.

"Forget Toulouse, then. It's seven-hundred miles to London. If you're any good at reading maps you can show me the quickest route. If you're very sure."

Isla did not dare hope, did not let herself fully take in the sight of the dappled light on his arms, or the heat in his eyes, or think about the warmth of that fingertip against her face. Instead, she tipped her head back towards the inescapable sun for a second, pretending to think. Her mind was quite still.

"What's the worst that could happen?" she smiled at him. "I'll read the map, you follow."

September | Hong Kong
Jennie Walmsley

"I'm sorry, I'm sorry, I'm sorry."
Mrs Tang regarded her with regal disdain, as if Katy's words of apology were cold, ungutted fish flopped down on the polished granite work surface beside the Duty Free bags. Katy pushed one of the bags towards Mrs Tang, who gave the merest hint of an acknowledgement with an arched eyebrow. Then the older woman flicked her cloth across the worksurface with the added emphasis of a loud nostril exhalation, grabbed the bag and stalked out of the kitchen.

Katy extracted a bottle of gin from one of the bags and poured a handsome measure into a glass. Tonic supplies were low, but she mixed the last flat dregs with imaginative splashes of pear and prune juice from the fridge: a cocktail, a 'Hong Kong Phooey' to mark her homecoming. A shame that Alec wasn't available to toast her return, but then being a Master of the Universe required constant vigilance and, so it had transpired after ten years of marriage, frequent absences from the home.

She glanced at her watch, just gone 9. The twins would have been lullabied to sleep with military precision by Mrs Tang two hours ago. She'd check on them later, after she'd spoken with Fiona.

There wasn't much Katy missed about England, certainly not the weather or the food, or the transport system, but she did miss Fiona's reassuring presence. The eight-hour time-difference made it difficult to have a good natter when both were 'off-duty'. But the 9 o'clock window was prime Fiona-time. Katy would dive into her first post-kids glass of Chardonnay, and Fiona could stride out from the solicitors in Henley through the bleak greys of a Thames lunch hour, their words volleyed back and forth across timezones by satellite.

Fiona answered immediately, slightly breathless, as if she'd been running, "Hi Babes, how're you doing?"

"Just back. No Alec, boys asleep, fire-breathing dragon snorting her way back to Sham Shui Po or wherever."

Katy had an ambivalent relationship with Mrs Tang. She found her genuinely, and unpolitically corrected, inscrutable. Mrs Tang had been with them for four years, since the beginning of Katy's pregnancy. She'd been an Amah before, had glowing references, and an irrefutable knack for predicting Katy's needs – from preparing Chinese herbal teas which reduced morning sickness, to providing gentle footrubs when oedema had caused Katy's feet to assume elephantine proportions in the later stages or pregnancy. Mrs Tang's English was perfunctory, and Katy's Cantonese equally limited, but nevertheless they'd found ways to communicate. But Katy didn't trust her. So much so, she'd followed her home one night, and discovered she didn't return to a highrise in Sham Shui Po after all, but rather travelled out to the New Territories by bus.

"It's not definitive proof she's a child-molester," Alec had responded when Katy had finally waddled into the flat with her news.

"No, but it's odd, Alec. Why was she going there? Some of the girls in the office say illegals live out near Sai Kung. It's not implausible she's an illegal."

Alec had nodded slowly, although he hadn't taken his eyes off the computer screen.

"It's not implausible, but neither is it implausible that Mrs Tang was going to visit her sister in the New Territories and that you've got an ever so slightly hormonally imbalanced imagination gland pulsing away over-actively, my sweet."

He'd stabbed the keyboard so violently that Katy realised he wasn't actually checking e-mails, but playing some evil online game instead.

"She wasn't carrying an overnight bag, and she hadn't come out by the time I left. I'm sure she's living there."

"Maybe she was visiting her lover."

Alec didn't take Katy's concerns seriously although he had offered to sack Mrs Tang for not necessarily sleeping at her stated home in Sham Shui Po, and therefore, possibly, being an illegal alien. Mrs Tang had stayed, but Katy was sure she didn't know everything about the woman who looked after her twin boys, and she often shared her uncertainties with Fiona.

"Dragon-breath wasn't very happy about last night. She was oozing frustration at having to do an impromptu sleepover. But we pay her extra for babysitting a night a week. And she got her bag of duty-free swag out of it."

"So how was the trip?"

"The usual round of tedium. Singapore was hot and boring. Saigon was hot and dirty. I got some good deals, though. Some nice new products for the spring range, I'll send you some samples"

"Thanks".

Phone tucked under one ear, glass in hand, Katy grasped her handbag, slid open the glass door onto the balcony, and stepped out into the dark, damp of the evening, sliding the glass door closed behind her.

"Listen, Fiona, I have something important to tell you. The reason I'm late getting back is because I met someone."

"What do you mean 'met'. As in 'met, met'?"

"I mean I *met* someone"

"As in the Biblical fashion of meeting? A meeting of parts, not just of minds? Oh my God. Where, when, how?"

Katy sat on one of the chairs next to the imposing dining table Alec had insisted they buy to furnish the balcony. They never ate out here – it didn't feel safe with the boys who were now of an age where they wanted to climb on everything. Katy only came out on the balcony for sneaky fags, which allowed her to admire the view, the unending parade of sparkling lights on the harbour, the Star Ferry ploughing backwards and forwards from this side to Kowloon.

Popping a Marlboro light between her lips, she lit it with deep relish, inhaling the evening.

"On the plane. He's an air steward with Singapore Airlines."

"You are kidding. Aren't all air stewards gay?"

"Nope and nope. He's been on the planes since he left college three years ago."

"Three years ago? Don't tell me he's mid twenties – you're becoming a dirty old woman, Katy."

"Twenty-six, but wise way beyond his years."

"He's not tall, dark and handsome too, is he?"

Katy watched the end of the cigarette crackle orange as she inhaled, "That and a lot, lot more. Look Fiona, I know this sounds strange, but he's different. There's something very special about him."

"What do you mean, 'special'?"

Fiona had clearly stopped walking now, and was sitting on a bench by the river, her attention fully focused on the conversation with her best and oldest friend. Someone she had known since their first day at primary school who was now six thousand miles away overlooking the dramatic nightscape of Hong Kong harbour.

Katy blew a film of smoke over the distant dark bays, out towards the islands where she didn't go frequently enough. She should take the boys there more. Out to Lamma for a picnic with some buckets and spades. It was too easy to find yourself driven by the city's relentless clock-watching.

"He knows things that he shouldn't know. He understands me in a way that I've never felt understood before."

"Hang on a minute, you know he knows you that well when you've known him how long? Last night on the flight?"

Katy flicked her cigarette over the edge of the glass screen and watched the tiny orange spark fall through the dark. So many people out there living infinitely small lives in their penthouses and flats, consuming, selling, buying. Each of the lights in the surrounding blocks an indication of an enclosed life: like grubs in the individual cells of a honeycomb.

"I met him last month on that first flight to Singapore. We knew we'd meet up again this week. I know it sounds strange, Fiona, but there's really something different about him. I mean unique. I think he's The One."

"Katy, I love you dearly, and you know I never want to curb your enthusiasm, but aren't you being hasty? I know things have been tough between you and Alec recently, but fundamentally he's not a bad man, you know, and even if he's not prepared to do another round of IVF, you can't blame him. It was pretty grim last time round. He's a good man really. A good dad at least. What's a late adolescent flight attendant in tight pants going to offer you that Alec can't?"

The question was finished with a snort of distant laughter from beside the Thames. Katy laughed at the same time, but not necessarily at the same thought. This was a single thread of conversation passing between people in different seasons: from heat and humidity to milky mist of autumn above the river. From night to day, soon from tomorrow to the day before. Two people in distinct timezones. Was it possible to talk across the divide? Katy sipped her drink. Number one superguy.

"It's not what you think. It started off flirtatiously enough, and you're right, when I first saw him I did have sad-old-dissatisfied-wife thoughts."

"Less of the 'old', thirty-eight is not old. Some of us haven't even got to the wife bit either."

Katy swirled the remains of the aubergine-coloured liquid in her glass, "OK. Anyway, I did have disreputable thoughts at first. Sex with Alec's lost some of the fizz now. I resent him so much. Somehow sex and fertility or infertility's all mixed up with Alec. It's me that would have to do all the injecting business again. Just one more go. Is it too much to ask? Isn't there something in this marriage business about giving your spouse what they want? We had a terrible fight before I went away – you know throwing ridiculous ultimatums at each other, you know, the ultimate sort. I wouldn't be surprised if he's disappeared off for another of his 'international conferences' and I don't see him again for weeks. It'll be a bloody miracle if we're still together this time next year. I don't feel the love, just his absence from me and the boys. Anyway, maybe that's what I found so attractive about Kelvin."

"The air steward is called 'Kelvin'?"

"That's his English name, yes. I admit it's a bit chavvy."

"'Kelvin' not really Dreamboy, Katy"

"Look stop teasing, he's not a Dreamboy. He's better than that. He's God"

Katy drained the dregs from her glass. She'd said it. She stood up to get a refill, sliding the glass door open onto a clean white kitchen of airconditioning.

"You mean he's divine?"

"Exactly. That's exactly what he is. I mean really. I think he is. He's God."

Ducks paddling their way through the brown leaves on the banks of the Thames hurled their derision down the phone line into the Hong Kong night. Katy could hear Fiona take a long, abnormally slow intake of breath, "Are you serious, Katy?"

"Yes. Really. Really, really serious. He is God. I mean the real deal, like Jesus Christ, only 21st century."

There was a long slow exhalation of breath down the line from Henley. Followed by a silence that seemed to span the globe and several millennia. The fridge hummed its scepticism in sympathy as Katy poured pineapple and mango juice into the gin this time.

"Look, Babes, I don't want to sound unduly doubtful, or disbelieving or whatever, but... an air steward on Singapore Airlines? I mean, it's hardly a venue for the Second Coming, is it? Who's he going to save? Depressed business travellers?"

Plink, plink, the ice from the freezer made satisfying plops in the drink. Katy kicked the fridge door shut and moved the phone from its uncomfortable position on her left shoulder back into the palm of her right hand.

"I agree, it's not what I would have imagined, either, but why not? I mean, what do you expect, a carpenter with a donkey on the West Bank?"

"Well, yes, maybe, I mean something a bit more relevant to, you know, world peace. Serving gin and tonics in Business class between Hong Kong and Shanghai isn't what I'd imagine God should be doing, even in his spare time."

"Which is possibly why he's got the job and we haven't," Katy held the sweaty, cold exterior of the glass to her temple which was throbbing. "Look I know it sound strange. But, why not? Why not God as an air steward?"

"It's not very pc, is it, Katy?"

"Neither was carving crucifixes in Jerusalem. I mean, we just can't know, Fiona, I can only tell you he convinced me."

"Well it's a great chat-up line, great or cheesy. 'Hi, I'm Kelvin, come fly me, and suck the cock of God.'"

Katy sighed. She perched on a stool next to the breakfast bar. On the shelves beside her were numerous photos of her and the twins, when they were babies, when they'd just come back from the hospital after three weeks in incubators. One of the photos showed their feet poking out from beneath blankets, with Katy holding up her right thumb in a "Great, thumbs up, gottem" sign and to give perspective on their fragility, her thumb nail hardly smaller than their tender wrinkled soles.

"I didn't suck his cock."

"Good, that would've been cheap. I think you should make even God wait. But, seriously, what did you do, then? How did he convince you?"

Katy had known this would be the difficult part. What had he said exactly, what had he done? They'd talked for most of the flight, at least for the parts when he wasn't serving the other passengers. He'd seemed to know lots about her instinctively. He'd called her by her name when she hadn't told him it. He could have taken that off a passenger list, of course. But he'd known she was travelling for business, that she was married, that she had small children.

"He could have surmised all that," Fiona chirped in merrily, tossing her crusts to the ducks. "I mean it's not rocket-science, Babes, wedding ring, certain age, bags under your eyes..."

The thing was not so much that he could identify her as a type but that he'd seemed to understand about her inner emotional turmoil. He'd offered to take her out for a drink, he'd meet her the other side of baggage collection.

"We went to his hotel for a drink."

"I can't believe I'm asking this, but where does the Messiah stay in Hong Kong?"

Katy snorted and smiled. She liked the combination of the mango and gin, it was beginning to soften her senses and help her relax, "The Mandarin, where else?"

"Singapore Airlines is doing well despite the economic downturn, then?"

He'd said the Singapore Airline staff always stayed at one of the major hotels in Hong Kong. Still the suite was quite impressive. He had his own living room with tasteful sofas, vases of lilies, a bathroom with floor to ceiling windows and views over the harbour. Better than you'd expect for an airline steward. But then Kelvin was better than you'd expect *of* an airline steward.

"Does God perform tantric sex?" Fiona's question seemed reasonable in its way.

"It wasn't about sex. It was about something deeper. He knew that I want to have more kids. That Alec and I have almost stopped talking to one another."

Fiona's scepticism was palpable the way it bristled down the phone line.

"He knew about you too."

"What did he know about me?"

"Where you live, what you do, your role in my life."

"How specific was he being? Did he know my name and my address? Is he some kind of weird stalker. You can find out an awful lot of stuff off the internet, Katy."

Katy slowly swept her free hand through her hair, the same way that Kelvin had done. It was as if he was inhabiting her hands, as if she could still feel his touch. She took another gulp of drink.

"I know, it was spooky. At first, it seemed like some sort of fortune-telling trick, but his insight was incredible. It was like being with someone who knew me really, really intimately. It was strange and when I realised he was for real, I didn't want to test him too much. But there was detail in the things he said."

"Like what?"

"He knew where I was born and that it was more than two days after mum's contractions began, and how she nearly died. He knew I had a horse when I was little, that I loved Pegasus more than anything, and how I fell off her and nearly died that time at the gymkhana."

"Well, I don't know about nearly died, Katy. It was a bad accident..."

"No, it was more than that. I did nearly die, don't you remember I had concussion and I'd broken my collarbone? When I was talking about it with him, I remembered that sense I had of floating away towards somewhere else. And anyway, don't you think it's strange he knew about that level of detail? You can't guess someone's childhood pet from their passport, and I've not posted any details like that on the internet..."

Katy began to dismantle the fruit bowl, sniffing every orange to check its ripeness. She felt she could detect the hint of the first white blush of mould that sometimes colonised the citrus fruit. She turned each clementine and lemon over, one by one, carefully checking their skins.

She knew how to read Fiona's silence, a cynicism that normally anchored her in reality, but which now suggested blindness.

"He knew details about you too. That you live alone. That you're an only child. He knew about your scars."

Katy swivelled the fruit bowl around, examining its glass surface, wiping imaginary smears off its surface with her thumb. There was a tiny inverted reflection of herself in the bowl's surface, a miniature pale spectre sitting in a blindingly white kitchen. She pushed the bowl back to its place next to her wedding photo, the one she had on display of her and Alec a lifetime ago, confetti catching them in laughter, for better for worse. Maybe she should go to bed. She was tired. She needed to sleep. Maybe it would be clearer tomorrow. Fiona was asking her something.

"What? Sorry Babes, I was daydreaming a moment, what did you say?"

"I asked, what he wanted from you, apart from the obvious? Why did he decide to reveal himself to you, this man who thinks he's Jesus flying around South Asia with a hostess trolley?"

Was there a slight hint of envy in Fiona's voice? A touch of something dark and disappointed with the sluggishness of life in Oxfordshire contrasted with the exoticisms of Hong Kong and the promise of an Oriental Saviour?

Katy smirked, "He said he wanted to save me, of course. I think he would have whipped me onto the next flight to Hanoi if I'd asked him. But I didn't. He did promise me it will be OK, though. He kept telling me to believe that it will be alright."

Her fingers rehearsed the circular movements his had traced on the back of her hand, over her wedding ring, as he'd talked about compromise, the seeming impossibility of achieving peace, the need for balance.

"What, did he go all cosmic on you, talk about Yin and Yang? Read your star signs? Perform any miracles?"

Katy sighed. She loved Fiona's sense of humour usually. Just now she felt wearied by it. "Well he did actually. One of the oldest in the book: water into wine. Swear to God when he poured it, it was Evian, but when I drank it, it was Chablis."

"Good, well I'm glad he's got style and still believes in the power of booze to convert. How 'bout something more significant – a resurrection, an immaculate conception?"

"He's not a performing seal, you know. But I know he's capable of those things, it's just there wasn't much call for a loaves-and-fishes routine on the flight." Katy knew it was unlikely. But why not? Why not a personal appearance by God for her, here in Hong Kong? Didn't God have infinite time to rescue people? Flip flop around time, answer their prayers, save them from despair? Why shouldn't he come in a blue blazer rather than an outfit of flowing robes which might excite the interest of Customs?

"Look, I do want to hear more, but I've got to go. I'm sure Kelvin is the One. He's right at least that things will be OK, I'm sure. Will you look after yourself, get yourself an early night? We can talk again tomorrow. Same time same place?"

They often hung up abruptly like this with one another on the phone. Their conversation an interminable one, that was merely interrupted by the rest of their lives needing to be conducted inconveniently, in different places. Over the years they'd got used to picking up where they'd left off. Tomorrow, no doubt Fiona would want more details about the night in the hotel. What did God wear in bed? Did he have a tummy button? She could already predict the jokes about the Second Coming.

Katy drained her glass, contemplated a third gin and then opted sensibly for a glass of cold water. She could be sensible if she needed to be. She stepped out of her heels and kicked them towards the doorway where Mrs Tang would pick them up in the morning. Kitchen light turned off, she padded down the corridor to the boys' room. Gentle snores indicated life beneath Oscar's duvet; Benedict's arms flopped wide over the edge of his bed. She'd leave them undisturbed.

In the bathroom, she fumbled for a spare toothbrush, her toiletry bag still in her suitcase. A packet fell off the medicine cupboard shelf into the sink. As she tore it open, she examined her eyes in the mirror, her bags were larger. The packet wasn't a toothbrush. She contemplated the plastic tube in her hand for a moment and then pulled her trousers and pants down and sat on the loo, thrusting the tube between her legs into the warm stream of wee. Fiona would be striding back to the office, coat collar turned against the breeze, digesting the news: the "Good News". Katy was saved. There is a God. It would all be alright. She would be OK. She pulled the plastic tube from between her legs and watched the blue line emerge in the window in the way photographic prints used to develop, an image, the future, revealing itself in the form of a slender blue line. A positive line.

At the threshold to her bedroom, she paused to feel for the light switch on the wall and then saw a figure lying in her bed. He rolled towards her in the half-light, throwing the duvet back to welcome her in. He was here after all. "You're back, I've been waiting." Alec's voice was sleepy and welcoming and forgiving. She clutched the plastic predictor in her hand like a crucifix as she slid into the bed next to him.

October | South Africa
Alexa Hughes Wilson

"Agh no man, it's not there."

"What the Hell?" Fritz banged one fist down on the front desk.

"It isn't there." Kobus repeated resignedly, but with eyes gazing blankly into his computer screen.

"You're joking; this is the fifth time this has happened since I've been working here – that's only three months." Fritz was annoyed. Another missing car; another tip down the drain. He had been at this Camps Bay hotel since mid July, waiting tables, taking a break from his travels around Southern Africa to stir up some more cash.

"Hey Kobus, how long have you been here? A year?"

"'Bout that."

"Aren't you beginning to wonder what's up with the cars?"

"Nope. Always the same rental agency, just incompetent: mixed up keys, mixed up contracts. Don't be paranoid, Fritz. There's enough to worry about that's real. If someone wants to steal a car from the garage, fine with me, just don't take me with it."

"OK then, you go tell our 'five-star' guests to be grateful their car is missing, since they didn't get their heads blown off in the process."

"Not my job, bru." Kobus grinned from behind the front desk, more amused to watch Fritz squirm than bothered about wrecking some spoiled tourists' day out at the Cape or wherever they were off to enjoy themselves.

Actually each time he found it incredibly funny, just a little welcome to Africa for all those saps who thought 'luxury travel' could really squeeze the chaos and danger out of this country.

Fritz just wanted his tips and to get back in his hiking boots. He turned to face the glass doors opening onto the terrace where his soon-to-be disappointed guests were finishing lunch in the dazzling October sun. A perfect day. Camps Bay's Atlantic waters sparkled as blue as the pool.

His eyes roamed table to table, couple to couple. They all seemed to be couples today, trying to have a perfect life. A five-star life. Quickly Fritz made a study of the man who would soon be yelling at him. Expensive-looking sunglasses, slight tan, too much smile, too white teeth. Expensive-looking wife. The man's hand kept moving from her tanned arm to her face, then to the back of her chair. Possessive. Just to put a smile on his face, he tried to imagine them at the end of a day's hike, parched, sweaty, sun-burned, with packs hanging from their shoulders. Fritz pushed through the glass doors, muttering, "He's going to be a nasty prick." But he was wrong about Jérôme Rastignac; he was never angry.

Approaching their table, trying to look slightly alarmed and embarrassed, Fritz announced, "I'm afraid the car has gone missing."
"Gone missing?" Jérôme smiled; his typical bemused expression caused one eyebrow to crinkle up and the other to crinkle down. He turned to his wife, "Do you think the luggage has 'gone missing' as well?"
"Actually sir, I'm sorry to say it has, since the valet stored it for you in the car this morning, as you requested."
"Let me try my luck again, has the bill also gone missing?"
He couldn't really help it, Serena knew. He had always loved his little moments of theatre. They used to seem so amusing to her, especially when they were played just for her. Serena met Jérôme's grin with a thin smile. If the car really had been lost, stolen, or otherwise put out of use, they would miss their first vineyard visit and it was the one she had found most difficult to arrange in the first place.

Now the slightly blushing waiter presented the bill for the night, breakfast, lunch and garage charge.
"You may want to remove the parking charge under the circumstances, but no hurry as we will be waiting here until some car is found, or perhaps you rent ponies or bicycles?"
"Certainly, sir. I will try to locate your car and bags... and adjust the bill."
Fritz turned on his heel and strode back inside with a little snarl in his throat. Serena blinked then looked up trying to make the tears stay where they were, stinging her eyes. Even if they got another car soon, she would be late for the first meeting at the vineyard she was most excited about buying from– first choice, first meeting for her first business. And

like so many things it seemed to have just slipped out of reach.

"Ma Sirène, not that face... it's a delay not a disaster."

Jérôme always called her that when she was sad or angry.

"Ma Sirène, call them and make a new appointment."

"Look J, this was the only day they had free for our whole visit. They have some consulting winemakers visiting from France this week so they were totally booked up, except this afternoon."

Her brittle voice surprised even her. All her hope suddenly felt quite fragile.

He took her hand, uncurled the fist and squeezed it.

"Pessimiste. Phone them. And if you can't meet, you can still buy their wine. Our friends just want something off the import radar for their restaurants. Surely you can just buy some bottles from them. Trust yourself."

"That's not the point – it's just a bad start."

Serena lifted her gaze up trying to stop the mood freefall that was emptying out her insides. This was supposed to be her part of the business. The rest was his: Jérôme's friends, their restaurants, his property. Jérôme's money, Jérôme's idea to pull her out of this place she was going right now. Stop. Stop. Stop. Stop.

"Pessimiste et superstitieuse, ma Sirène?"

He was wrapping her hand around his phone.

Serena pulled out her folder with all the contacts she had arranged, found the number, sighed and dialed. Her husband's eyes tracked the conversation. Not good news. The two visiting winemakers had gone missing from a vineyard the day before, causing complete chaos. They couldn't make any appointments and preferred not having any visitors until the matter was settled, just as a safety precaution.

"No, not a pessimist, not superstitious." Serena turned her gaze toward Camps Bay and sent her siren self back to the water. She took a deep audible breath and got up from the table, "I'm going to go arrange a car."

And she did. An hour later they were heading down to see the Cape of Good Hope with a driver and car the hotel manager had pulled out of a hat. Their rental car and luggage were still missing, but again the manager had assured her they would be delivered to their next hotel by the evening, and they could keep car and driver until that time. Now that the day's meeting was off, she had decided to enjoy the fine spring weather, some sites, maybe spot whales.

The drive down was stunning. It lifted both their spirits watching the coast unfold with its dramatic rocks and crashing waves. In a calm cove they even caught a glimpse of cape zebras grazing. Their conversation turned to the project at hand. It had begun as a chat with some friends who were opening a restaurant. Serena asked them about their chef and the wines. They were pulling the chef from a sinking restaurant they loved and were in the midst of wrestling with various wine suppliers. This opened up a little rant against all the boring wines that appeared again and again on every menu. Jérôme, always full of ideas and plans, eyed Serena. She had spent years selling wines in restaurants and chain stores, but the subject still made her face light up. Why not start importing small selections from a few young producers? Branding them for the restaurant trade with the possibility of expanding in the retail market?

He had piles of connections in the food world and complete confidence in Serena's nose. She seemed to live one step closer to the world than anyone else he had ever known; she smelled it, felt it and saw it with an immediacy that riveted her. Sometimes he felt like a blind man hearing the world through her voice, but lately that voice had faded to a whisper. By the following morning, Jérôme had drafted a business plan and had sent e-mails, bolting forward with ideas and pulling Serena out from under the covers. For about a year she had been entangled in this lethargy, a dangerous siren song that threatened to drown her spirit. Now he hoped a project together would call her back to life.

They had settled on South African wines to start with, after considering her local California wines or wines from his beloved South of France. Jérôme had friends in Cape Town who could help connect them to small producers and then Serena could sniff out the jewels that had not yet reached the export market. A few months later they had made a first trip out to meet people, taste wines, and bring back some samples. With his swagger and Serena's enthusiasm, they had won over some truly talented winemakers. This time they were back to finalise selections and nail down terms. The fact that their favourite small vineyard and first appointment had fallen through wouldn't stop them. Already they had confirmation, that morning, of most other meetings, including some invitations to stay on for lunch at several locations. Now Serena's eyes flashed as she began talking through the wines they would be revisiting, remembering the characters that went with them and the scents around their vineyards and cellars.

When they reached the Cape Nature Reserve, their driver stopped and invited them to stroll the paths while he waited. All the guidebooks recommended taking in the views and seeing the thousands of native plants, but once they were up on the cliffs with two oceans tumbling below, surrounded by unrecognisable flora, they finally experienced the overwhelming majesty of the Cape. Jérôme loved capturing these moments when Serena was totally immersed in observation, down on her hands and knees poking at the fynbos with all its unfamiliar leaves and flowers, spying dassies scurrying away or lost to the horizon. The gestures were tender, both his and hers, but parallel. Serena turned to look at Jérôme's camera face, and thought how far away he seemed and how much less alone she would feel if she had been sitting by herself with only the silently creeping, tiny tortoise for company. She wanted to tell him to put down the camera and come sit by her, and simply watch the little flickerings of colourful insects making their way on the ground. And yet her tongue was like a stone in her mouth. He smiled his enormous bright smile, "Ma Sirène, we should go back."
It struck her that his smile was like the camera; it pushed the world away one step so that he never seemed to be quite where she was, even when they touched each other. She reached her hand out to his and he pulled her up from the ground, still smiling. Letting go of her hand, he headed back to their driver. Serena followed a few paces behind.

When they reached the car, their driver informed them that their rental car had been located and delivered with the luggage to their hotel in Stellenbosch. The only complication was that he needed to bring the man who had brought their car back to Cape Town as soon as possible, so they would not take the full scenic tour, but drive directly to the wine country. Slightly relieved and slightly disappointed, the couple hopped in the car and began looking through the pictures Jérôme had just taken. Later on, they would sort through and identify the plants, make prints, frame them and hang them in their bedroom, which in two years had taken on the air of a Victorian horticultural collection. They each appeared in the photos only as fingertips or shadows. Now with their eyes focused on the little images at the back of the camera, they lost track of their progress toward Stellenbosch, until they noticed a second and a third U-turn on a tiny road that seemed to be dwindling in the sand. The driver was obviously lost. His mate had tried to describe a shortcut, he explained, but now he couldn't find the road and his phone had lost reception.

Serena felt her stomach turn into a knot and her right hand go numb. What kind of driver gets lost on his home turf? There were a few shacks on the road ahead and Serena began to wonder whether this was all planned from the start, with their car and belongings being stolen, and then... what next? A fisherman was walking past the car as they made yet another turn. Serena pushed the button to roll down her window and waved to get the man's attention. She just managed to open the door and to start to put one foot out when the driver accelerated violently. The door swung back on her ankle and Jérôme pulled her into the car. Her sense of panic rose and spilled out in a torrent. She heard herself shouting at the driver and at Jérôme, but her voice felt as if it came from someone else because her own voice was frozen in fear.

The driver looked back at both of them for a quick moment, then turned his eyes to the road. His voice was steady. "I am a man of God; I am a Christian. I will not harm you or lead you into harm if I can help it. This is a mistake not a kidnapping so stay calm, please. You did not see the knife at that man's side. That and his eyes made me speed away. In life, this is how I survive, but today I have made a mistake. A safe road is better than a short road and now we are lost in a rather dangerous place. The windows must stay up and we cannot stop; anyone here will notice this is a rental car and expect tourists with money. If we are stopped, get down on the floor of the car; I have a gun and will do my best to protect you. For now please just stay quiet."

Jérôme replied, "Thank you for your chivalry, but I am sure we will all be fine." And then he smiled.

Serena wanted to shout at him or slap the smile from his face. She felt like she was facing a phantom guillotine on a desert island in the company of the Chehsire cat. She was afraid and completely alone, so she bit her lip and looked out the window at the waves some distance away. Serena almost wished they were being kidnapped; she wanted to see if Jérôme could be changed by fear for himself, or even for her.

At this point the anxious driver began searching, not for the right road, but simply for a larger road; something that might eventually take him where he would find his bearings. Jérôme was searching the back of Serena's head. When you have been married for even a few years, you can read fear and anger simply in the line of the shoulders, the glimpse of chin. He wondered when she had lost her mad courage that had drawn him to her only four years ago. If he had shown the courage to ask her, she would have replied that solitude had drained it from her. She would have claimed that courage is theatre even if performed only for ourselves. And now, though he watched her all the time, she felt vanishingly distant, small, solitary.

About the time the driver found a road he knew, his phone rang. Even though Jérôme only understood half the words, he knew the other driver was receiving such an onslaught of abuse that Jérôme actually felt sorry for him. He knew how fear makes some people so angry, but he simply didn't feel it anymore. For him it wasn't courage that kept him calm, he thought, and then he left the thought alone, suspended in the past. In that past he was a young man holding a woman while she died at the side of the road, twenty years ago. He turned back to the camera where he flicked again through the day's photos and waited for Serena.

Not until they reached the beautiful entry to Lanzerac did Serena's body soften back into the seat. The yellow evening sun stretching across the lawn thawed her features. The buildings were stunningly white, such a stark contrast to the green of grass, oak, and vine. Such a contrast to everything black in the rich soil that was the source of vitality for the shimmering surface. She couldn't change it, any of it. They had chosen an easy place to stay, to entertain if the situation arose, yet now it felt so ridiculously gorgeous and exclusive, so touristic. Serena felt guilty that she had not bothered to sort out the travel details. Jérôme's assistant had, but had put them all in the name Mme. Rastignac, her married name. God, now she flogged herself for the empty hours spent in bed while the phone rang at 8am. Of course his assistant had chosen this New York Times approved beauty. Oh it was up-and-down and up-and-down. The gloriously perfect, white manor house and outbuildings in Cape Dutch style were made for him, she thought, not her. She had never asked for the slick gloss of perfection. Before, she could have handled lost cars as part of the chaos of life's travels, but now as Mme. Rastingac every little detour threatened to shatter her sense of safety. Who was this terrified woman, she wondered, listening to the gravel crunch beneath the tires? Serena had always liked the grit of adventure, but now felt boxed into something like an American Express brochure travel advert.

Jérôme swept open the door to reception. The rich mahogany desk made her nervous: "Yes, Mme. Rastignac. For five nights; a suite. Royal pool?"
"Yes, I think so."
"Can the valet take your bags?"
"No, we have no bags. Or maybe... Have they arrived before us?"
"So sorry, let me check... Yes, I am sorry, not to have noted this. They are in your room. May the valet show you to the room? Oh, but before you go, may I reserve a table for you in the restaurant for tonight? Your original request was unclear."
Serena found herself looking to Jérôme. She was tired and would have liked to swim in the Royal pool and collapse in the arms of the mini bar. "8:30 if that is not too late," he replied, blithely unaware of how she felt like melting under the water and the covers with him, like swimming out of her icy fear into the smell of his neck, into his smell, something familiar and earthy of him that belonged to her. Instead there would be dinner.

They had two hours to go before dining and suddenly they seemed to Serena to be waiting for her, as they entered the huge, luxurious suite. She quickly stripped off her clothes and plunged in the chilly pool outside the doors of their bedroom. Each moment under the water absorbed all the electricity that the day had left in her body, until after about ten minutes, she felt utterly limp. Next she filled the enormous bath with water which rushed in all rusty-red and boiling. She could have complained, but couldn't be bothered to find the phone and wait to be advised to shower. She just wanted to be submerged in warm water and feel herself floating in the comfort of her own chosen liquid solitude. Half an hour later she emerged, lobster pink with puckered fingers, ready to place herself in the bed next to Jérôme. It was a habit they had from early days of travelling together, when she was amazed at all the comforts beyond a Motel 6. They would make love then dine, because they were lucky, because they were both lucky and in love and sexy and happy and attracted and fertile and new and unstoppable. Now they still had sex in each new bed before dinner, despite all the other adjectives that had fallen by the wayside. Then, after, she would choose what to wear down to dinner. OK, she thought about it while they lay in bed because she couldn't think what else to think about at first...

And what she felt? Surprisingly, tonight she felt hope after the swim and bath. Maybe it was her anger that had taken her out of some sexual lethargy, but after playing near dead for too long she felt a sharp longing pull up inside her like a cord. Jérôme had given up, when suddenly, his hands gently resting against her fur had awakened the relief of fear, and she wanted to fuck out all the anguish of thinking they would die, of being alone and afraid. She pushed her bum back and tucked his fingers into her body just the way she needed them. The last year disappeared, and she felt her body a gift and his body a pleasure. She used them both in every way she wanted and then in every way he wanted. When she finally needed to bite at his lips and press her head against his, he pushed her over, carefully watching for any resistance in her curled lip, but no, it was curling otherwise... Once on top of her, Jérôme let Serena pull his hands back inside her, and felt her other hand gently push him inside her tightest curves. Having given him all the invitation he needed, she then shook against the painful press of his body cramming into her; she bit his fingers and he crushed his legs against the flesh of her tensed thighs. They came, then she came again.

Afterwards she and Jérôme had a first glass of wine from the room's fridge: the Lanzerac fizz. She searched for some CDs in the hotel's offering and smiled over the slightly worn but lovely jazz tunes: "Paper

Moon," "A Kiss to Build a Dream on..." Now she thought to herself that it could all go... the distance, the anger... there was everything there, yes, to build a dream on and her smile reached out to her lover. He smiled, impenetrable as ever: happy, bon vivant, faraway.

As they walked to the door of the suite, she twirled in her unusual high-heels and tea length skirt that shimmered; she felt a tiny bit drunk after only one glass, oh two, of fizz. She gave a laugh and called Jérôme her petit chou, which she always said badly and made him laugh. They were both still laughing as they entered the elegant dining room of the Lanzerac Hotel. As a lark, she twirled in the door, because she was still herself, not really Mme. Rastignac, whatever his assistant had said in the reservation. MME. RASTIGNAC: table for two.

Jérôme still loved these dining rooms even after years of finding them: it still always felt like a surprise, and he loved seeing that in Serena's eyes; her nervousness, her audacity, her pleasure in the luxury he pretended not to see. One could say it made him feel powerful, but he would say it made him feel grateful. Serena saw it both ways, but mostly only saw what was before her: the candles, nicely upholstered chairs, tall glasses and Jérôme's smile.

He sensed the two dangerous peaks of anger and pleasure, and watched the river that would divide them flowing into their glasses: a welcome drink. It would all be too much because outside of sex, Jérôme wouldn't be able to get back to her, so she would be alone. Then it would just be wine and the memory of fear and the song of la Sirène. But that would be later. For now it was laughter and amuse-bouches, golden glasses with golden bubbles and candle glow and words, words, words.

Serena loved to talk when she was happy. She reviewed the wine list and was thrilled to see very few of their picks included. She wanted new wines, new winemakers, new flavours. And new plants. She wondered about trying to grow some of the astounding flowers from the Cape back in California. The climate should suit. She chatted through all the details of the day without mentioning any of the things that had gone wrong, yet somehow Serena kept hearing her fears as if whispered into her ear: 'terrified', 'last moments', 'blindfolded', 'no escape'. Finally she leaned close to Jérôme, as if speaking ever so quietly would sequester the thought, and asked if he had just heard someone say 'tied-up for hours'. He gave her a very quizzical look and shook his head. Moments later, she glanced over at a table in an alcove on the other side of the restaurant, and realised that the vaulted ceiling was throwing their quiet conversation straight to her. As she listened, she recognised two of the faces at the table.

"J, it's them. The couple we couldn't meet this morning, but the missing ones are there. It must be them. They're all there; they're OK." Her eyes filled with tears of empathic relief.
"Of course, I told you it would be fine and we can see them, probably even tomorrow." He stretched his hands out across the white tablecloth to stroke the inside of her wrists, as he always did to calm her.
Serena stared across the table at Jérôme, enraged by his empty reception of this good news. She had wanted to walk over, offer drinks, toast their safe return and plan to meet. Instead, goose bumps crawled up her arms and silence clamped her jaws. Serena's whole body went rigid as it tried to swallow back the words gushing from her insides.

Her eyes fell to a circular shadow at the base of her wine glass and she pushed it ever so slightly back and forth, intently watching the shadow fluctuate. Jérôme's hand reached forward to brush the straight dark strands back from her face, but her eyes were fixed on the disc beneath her glass. Moments passed before she slowly lifted her gaze to his, and still her mouth stayed utterly motionless except for a slight throbbing in her lower lip. She heard the sound of her whole shell shatter with the room and Jérôme's face. He had been right: the wine, the fear, the day had broken her. Now harsh words came easily, quietly. The word "ineluctable" hovered around her brain like a fly at noon, but she spoke over it. She would not be fated to a life she could change.
"You are impossible. This is impossible. Totally impossible! You aren't blasé, calm, refined. You don't give a damn about any of us, do you?"
She waited for something to stop her, a look, a defence, a hand to her chin to drag the throbbing from her lip and pounding from her chest. Jérôme sat back slightly in his chair to examine his watch and twist his

cuff links. His nails needed cutting.

"Jesus J, you are emotionally deformed!"

He began to speak to his left cuff link, fluidly at first.

"Ma Sirène, what you don't know is that I can see how it all works out. Years ago I had the privilege of feeling fear and now feeling is replaced with knowledge which is so much less rich. A long time ago I watched all the colour drain from my life."

Jérôme paused to examine each nail on his left hand, then closed his fist and locked his other hand around it in a tight ball which he began tapping against his chin. He stilled his hands and spoke again, but this time slowly as if his mouth wanted to feel the articulation of every sound issuing forth.

"I watched her face... I sat... in that ditch... and held..." Here he began tapping again. "I could only watch." He sucked in his breath sharply and exhaled, blowing into his closed fist. "The police had found the driver, but never even looked... for another... I had seen the lights pass by... I was meant to meet them only a few miles on. When I saw the car and asked for the passenger, we began searching. No one imagined she could have been thrown that far. When I saw..." Tap. Tap. Tap. Tap. "When I saw her... I don't even know. If anything one person holds inside can give another one life in one look, in one instant... To try to give..."

Tap. Tap.

Then his words began to flow again, a painful half smile played at the corner of his mouth.

"My world went black. The world I came back to... is not your world, but you gave me a glimpse, renewed. I see too much and can change nothing. I prefer your eyes to mine, but mine will always be what you call ... what you call cold."

Here he looked up into Serena's green-gold ignited eyes.

"I invite you to stay for years because I see them all in you and through you, but strangely I cannot see if that could be with me."

For the first time in their years together, he looked stricken and she knew she couldn't be just eyes and that he knew it too.

The acoustics were such that the other table had grown silent and watched a man who could see the future, see the future.

November | Kenya
Lucy Cavendish

The tinny sound of Madonna's 'Holiday' can just be heard through Emma's earphones. Jon has been trying to ignore it for the past hour but, in all honesty, it has been driving him mad. He turns and looks at Emma. She is sitting there, earphones on, eyes closed, seemingly asleep. But Jon can see she is almost imperceptibly tapping her left foot to the beat. He reaches his hand out to touch her on the arm.

Emma's head snaps round, her eyes rapidly opening. 'WHAT?' she says, way too loudly.

'Your iPod,' mouths John. 'Too loud.'

'WHAT?' Emma yells again.

The woman in front of her turns and glares at Emma through the gap in the seats.

Jon leans over to take her headphones off.

'It's too loud,' he says to her, 'I can just hear the bass bit. It's irritating the woman in front of you.'

Emma blushes.

'Sorry,' she says.

'I can't sleep,' says Jon

'Did you want to sleep?'

'Well, yes.'

'OK,' she says. Then she turns away from him and starts digging around in her handbag, 'What's the name of the hotel we're staying at again?' she says.

As soon as they hit the runway, Emma knows she is in a foreign country. Not just foreign in the way that Italy might be foreign or maybe Greece but really, truly foreign. Everything is different, even the light. Emma stares out of the window as the plane's brakes judder to slow down. She can see a few black faces dotted around, staring at the great slab of metal now coming to a halt. She sees a boy, perhaps only about five years old, standing next to a few raggedy goats. He has a short thin stick in his hands and nothing on his bottom half. He just looks at the aeroplane Emma is sitting in as if he can't really see it. On the other side of him is the sea, a huge expanse of azure blue with bedraggled windblown palm trees lining the shoreline. It makes Emma sigh. This bleached-out place is Africa. It suddenly all seems so real.

An hour ago, all she could see through the morning mist hanging way down below her, was vast tracts of dry land as the aeroplane skimmed over the roof of the sky. She had marvelled at Africa then, at how animals she had only ever seen in the zoo were running free thousands of feet below her. Down there, she thought, are lions and zebra, giraffe and wildebeest. Down there people live in huts and struggle for survival. Up in the sky, she knew she and Jon knew nothing of that. They were just a newly married couple off on honeymoon. How weird the world is, thought Emma.

Jon is the first one off his seat. Emma knew he would be. He is always like this; eager, willing, ready for a challenge. Sometimes Emma thinks Jon should learn to walk before he runs. She says this to him and he always laughs at her.
'It's the kind of thing a mother says to a child,' he says, grinning.
Emma follows him to the door of the aircraft. The heat hits her in the chest. It's almost like a blow it is so forceful. Emma takes a great big gulp of hot, dry air in surprise. The boy with the goats is standing on the runway now, accompanied by a few donkeys.
'Welcome to Lamu,' says the pilot, coming out of his cabin. *'Habari malaika. Na cu penda mailaika.'*
He then laughs, 'ha ha ha ha ha!' and he reminds Emma of the villain from a James Bond film, the one who comes out of the grave and performs a witch doctor dance.
'Weird guy,' says Jon as he and Emma walk to the ferry that will take them across the waters of Manda island to the main town in Lamu.
By the time Emma reaches the boat, she is sweating. She sits on a bench and tries not the think about the diesel fumes she is inhaling. Instead, she looks down at the sea. The water is clear. She can make out rocks below them.
The boy gets on the ferry. A goat and a donkey follow him.

'They put animals on the ferry!' says Emma.

'Well, how else do they get across,' says Jon, putting on his Rayban Wayfarers and leaning his face into the sun.

'But they really smell,' says Emma, wrinkling her nose.

The boy stares dolefully at Emma again. She smiles at him. His face doesn't move a muscle.

'Jon, doesn't he remind you of someone?'

'No,' says Jon yawning. He reaches over and touches her knee. 'Christ Em. We are in Africa. That's amazing isn't it?'

'Yes,' says Emma simply, but she is not looking at him. She is staring at the boy with the goats.

Twenty minutes later, as the sun rises higher in the sky and Jon seems to have gently nodded off, his head lolling to one side as the boat climbs up each wave, falls and climbs up again, Emma remembers who this boy reminds her of. She has seen a child like him before. It was one night when she and Jon were walking back from a gig. Jon was slightly drunk. He decided he wanted a packet of fags so they stopped at a garage in Islington to get some. As Jon went into the shop, Emma hung back. There was a car in the forecourt. In the back of the car was a boy, sitting without any expression, staring at Emma out of the window. Emma gave the boy a small wave. She wasn't sure why. She just felt that maybe it would make her more friendly, but the child just carried on staring. It was then that Emma saw something silver glinting in the front of the car near the steering wheel. The keys were still in the ignition. Emma couldn't believe it. She looked round for the child's parent. She could see a man in the shop leafing through the magazines. Emma suddenly felt incensed. What on earth did that man think he was doing? Christ, anybody could get in that car and drive off and he'd be stuck at the bloody magazine counter, unable to do anything about it.

'Look!' Emma said, waving her hand angrily in the direction of the car as Jon reappeared.

'What?' said Jon, smiling as he tried to open the packet of Camel he'd just bought.

'That child is in the car on its own!'

'And?' said Jon, putting a cigarette in his mouth and walking off down the street.

'And anyone could drive off with it! Anyone. The keys are in the ignition and...'

Just then Emma heard the car start up. She wheeled around and saw the magazine-counter man in the driving seat about to move off.

'Why are you so bothered?' said Jon, searching in his pockets for a lighter.

'Why am I so bothered? Oh, I don't know. Maybe because children who are left alone go missing you know.'

'Oh no. Not the Madeline McCann conversation again. I thought we'd been through that one and agreed to disagree.'

'Yes but this is irresponsible Jon. Surely you must see that. Madeleine went missing and this boy could have easily been abducted. Why on earth would a father take that risk?'

'I guess it was his risk to take.'

'But what if someone had driven off with the boy? He'd be eaten alive with guilt!'

'Not necessarily. I mean, I wouldn't."

Emma stopped and turned to look at Jon.

'You're just drunk,' she said.

Later on, as they lay in bed, Emma believed that things had changed for her. In some ways she knew the conversation had got out of hand. They had argued for hours and yet it had all been so futile. Emma had screamed at Jon. She had cried. She railed at him. But Jon had merely sat on the sofa and told her he 'didn't do guilt."

'I don't believe in it. I would take responsibility for my actions but I would not feel guilty.'

'Christ Jon, only children don't feel guilt. Are you telling me you are the same as a child?'

Jon had merely smiled at her. He might as well have put his fingers in his ears and said 'la, la, la'. Emma wanted to hit him harder than she'd ever want to hit anyone.

She looks at him now so fast asleep, the sun on his face, his sunglasses drooping down his nose.

I want more in my life, she thinks. I want an adult, not a child.

The thought gives her the jitters.

As the ferry ploughs on through the water, the local dhows buzz around the boat like swallows swooping to pick off insects. Emma finds herself fascinated by the dhows. They look so free with their big billowing sails, manned by no one but the small, lithe, brown, muscular men darting around, steering them through the waves. Emma loves the structure of the boats – the roughly-hewn wood tied together with rope and a few rusty nails. She is amazed how fast they go, how sleek they are. She watches them as they scud across the waves, full of white tourists clad in nothing but bikinis, small swimsuits, speedos and sarongs. The tourists laugh and wave. They are drinking coconut juice from large, green coconuts whose tops have been sliced off with sharp pangas.

Without Emma realising it, Jon has woken up. He watches her closely. He turns towards her, takes her hand and starts to close his eyes again. He can see Emma as a blur, those features he knows so well, her pretty button nose, her little pinkish mouth, those tendrils of blonde hair curling round her face. If he closes his eyes just a little bit more maybe all her features will melt into one image of the woman he loves. Jon smiles. This is his Emma, the woman he has been married to for just less than a month. Emma, his wife, to have and to hold... Then he remembers how cross she was with him on the aeroplane.
'I never ask you to turn your iPod down,' she had said brusquely to him, turning away.
'For better or for worse,' Jon had replied, smiling. He is used to Emma's unexpected bad moods. Still, he would rather their marriage start off better. He sees Emma looking at the dhows and suddenly it comes to him. He will book them a day on a dhow. Emma will love him if he does this. He doesn't know why but he knows it's true.

The harbour at Lamu town is bustling with people. There are small girls selling bananas, and equally small boys running around shouting and screaming, and occasionally diving madly from the walls next to the harbour, emerging from the sea with shiny heads as sleek as seals. Occasionally a flash of colour appears in the crowd as sarong-clad tourists battle their way through. Local women, dressed top-to-toe in black but with intricately hennaed hands, sell small packets of roasted cashew nuts. One of them presses some into Jon's hand. He laughingly gives her a small bow which somehow irritates Emma.

'Pay her!' she hisses at him. She can see how the children have ragged clothes and no shoes, how the women's teeth are brown and rotten. There are donkeys everywhere. In fact, the whole harbour smells of donkey dung and something else, something fishy and rotten. Once they have negotiated their way out of the harbour, Jon pulls out a map. Small children, suddenly noticing the map, appear and crowd round them desperately trying to grasp the handles of their luggage.

'Me take you hoteli,' they keep saying to Emma, grinning their toothy grins and pulling at her clothes. '*Na wenda wapi?*'

'Put the map away,' Emma says tetchily to Jon. 'I can't stand much more of this hassle.'

Another boat pulls up just further along the water's edge. It is a graceful wooden dhow. It glides slowly into place and then stops, as if by magic, and disgorges a dozen tanned, young people, about the same age as Jon and Emma, onto the harbourside. Emma watches as a slim, blonde woman, clad in only a bikini top and hot pink shorts, brushes her way past the children who have suddenly raced over to sell her and her companions coconut juice.

'Juicy! Juicy!' they shout. The girl smiles at them all and just raises her hand.

'Asante sana,' she says and walks on looking as cool and unhassled as Emma feels hot and bothered. Behind her loiters a very good-looking blond man who is wearing a bandana. He reaches into his pockets and hands out coins to the boys.

'Asante sana,' they say, mimicking the girl. 'You good man. Where you stay good man?'

'Peponis,' he says, laughing.

'Ah, cool dude,' say the boys.

'For God's sake let's get to the hotel,' says Emma to Jon tetchily.

Once there, Emma sits in a large leather chair in the reception while Jon checks them in.

'Yes, Mr and Mrs Carrington,' she hears him saying proudly. She feels a small pang of guilt then. She knows why she is cross though. She had willed Jon to book the right hotel. From the moment he has suggested Lamu as their honeymoon destination, she had wanted to stay at

Peponis. She had seen it in the Kenya guidebook she has bought. She would read it at work when she was bored, which was quite a lot of the time. Instead of making endless calls to PRs and agents and people's people, she'd sit and read the book under the desk and that is when she saw the description of Peponis.

'Peponis is not only a hotel, it is *the* hotel. It is the only five-star hotel on the island of Lamu. Everyone who is anyone stays at this laid-back hotel.' Emma's heart thrilled when she read that. She imagined herself there, on the beach, staying in the right hotel, drinking the right drinks with the right people. Instead of being the celebrity booker for a half-baked daytime television chat show, she'd be up there, even above the C-list whose nightmarish habits and demands she had to cope with day in, day out. She had even imagined what she would wear. She paid a visit to Heidi Klein to invest in a tiny bikini even though she could not really afford it.

But of course Jon hadn't booked Peponis on the beach. He'd booked another hotel in the town described as 'hip and cool' by Emma's guidebook.

'Hey, it looks great doesn't it?' Jon had said, showing Emma pictures on-line of the type of place Emma thought backpackers with a little bit of money might stay. There were photographs of young white men in straw hats strumming guitars on a roof. They all looked as if they needed a good shave.

Emma looks at Jon. Now she comes to think of it, he looks as if he needs a good shave too. In fact, in many ways Emma thinks he looks exactly the same as he had when they were at university together. She can see he is as handsome now as he was then, with his dark hair, slim physique and brown eyes. He was the Ents officer when they were at Leeds together and, for a while, Emma was attracted and repelled by him at the same time. Everywhere she went, there he was putting on some band in order to support the eco-protesters in Nigeria or to help the Kurds gain independence. Although his energy made her feel nervous, Emma found herself also attracted to him. She admired his zealous nature although she was never sure who it benefited – him or the one-legged women in Congolese refugee camps.

One night she found herself with him towards the end of a gig. She had offered to stay and help clear up. She cannot remember who was playing. She just remembers sitting on the floor of an over-crowded room in the corner amongst the fag butts and ashes, talking to Jon. He always tells her that's when he fell in love with her. He tells her that's when she fell in love with him but she doesn't agree. It took another five years for them to get together and by then they'd both had their hearts broken by other people anyway.

Now they are married and she is here in this hotel with him. Jon comes over and takes her by the hand.
'To the bridal suite,' he says to her. 'Oh, and I have a surprise for you.'
'What, now?' asks Emma, slightly nervously.
'No Mrs Carrington,' he says. 'Tomorrow. You're going to love it.'

The next morning, Jon goes down to the main pier and asks how to get a dhow for the day. But he is there too late. Most of the dhows have gone. All he can find is a boy who looks about fifteen at the most. Jon tells him he needs a dhow, now, today.
'It's very important,' he says.
The boy tells him his name is Ali. He can take Jon out.
'What you?' Jon says incredulously. 'How can someone of your age have his own dhow?'
'Not mine,' says Ali. He tells Jon he knows someone who can. 'Where do you want to go?' he asks.
Jon shrugs. He doesn't know. He points vaguely out to sea.
Suddenly he finds himself telling Ali he has just got married.
'My wife wants it,' he says. 'I want to treat her.'
Ali nods and smiles.
'Be here in half an hour,' he says.

Half an hour later Jon is there with Emma. Emma is looking nervous – and very much like a new tourist. Her blonde hair is carefully tied back, skin white and smeared with sun cream. She is wearing a sun hat and carrying a wicker bag. In it she has a book and a sarong. She hasn't dared venture out from the hotel in anything as daring as only a bikini and sarong so she has on a thin white sun dress. She is wearing her brand new red bikini underneath it.

Although she is nervous, she is also excited. She can hardly believe that Jon has done this. She was in bed with the fan whirring above her head when Jon burst in and told her to get dressed. His enthusiasm was infectious.

'What is it?' she had asked him.

'We're going on a dhow!' he said and then he kissed her, he was so happy.

Jon and Emma wait on the pier until Ali sails up in a dhow. He is on his own bar a boy who seems about six years old.

'My brother Hamid,' he says. 'He can sail with me real good.'

Jon raises an eyebrow but Hamid nods vigourously.

'Is that it?' asks Emma in a worried voice. 'Is it just you and your brother?'

'We do this all the time,' says Ali cheerfully. 'You no believe me?'

Emma looks to sea – there are dhows everywhere skidding around and glinting in the sun. Jon follows her gaze. He decides quickly.

OK,' he says and they get in. Ali tells them it is his uncle's dhow as Emma and Jon settle down.

'My uncle wouldn't let me take this boat if I couldn't sail it,' he says.

Hamid just stares at them unblinkingly.

What is it with these unblinking boys thinks Emma.

Two hours later and Jon and Emma have finally relaxed. They are scudding along, blue sky, wonderful sea, peace and quiet. They sit and hold hands. Occasionally Ali says something to Hamid in a dialect that neither Jon or Emma understand and Hamid reaches into a cool box and hands them each a beer. Jon even lights up a cigarette when Ali offers him one of his own. Emma would usually be cross about this as Jon is not supposed to smoke but today, she laughs. She snuggles down into Jon's armpit. He tilts his head down and kisses her.

'I have something to tell you,' she says to Jon when he has stopped kissing her.

'What?' he says, dragging on the cigarette some more and blowing the smoke into the wind. 'You're not pregnant already are you?'

'No. Don't be silly! I just want you to know that I don't want to be a

researcher forever.' For some reason just saying this makes her giggle.
'No?' says Jon laughing with her. 'Because I obviously thought you did.'
'Do you know what my day consists of?' she says, now almost convulsed.
'I have to spend all my time chasing crap celebrities to come on the crap show I work for. Isn't that madness? My God, I could be here with you forever.' Suddenly she stands up. 'FOREVER!' she says loudly.
'Miss, stand down please,' says Ali smiling but his eyes look worried.
'Sorry,' she says.

An hour later they are becalmed. Ali is fishing and showing Emma how to haul the kingclip in. The idea is to get enough fish to eat then carry on sailing over to Manda, cook the fish with coconut rice and then come home. As Emma is fishing she notices the sea becoming choppy. She doesn't think about it. She and Jon have had a few beers now. The sun is high. Emma catches a fish and yelps.
'I have one! I have one!'
Jon raises his thumb up at her and yawns.
'Sleepy boy!' Emma calls out to him. Jon laughs.
Just then another dhow scuds past. The good looking blond man from the day before is in the boat. He sees Emma, who is now in her bikini and sun hat, standing there holding her fish. He waves at her. Emma waves back. The man lets out a playful whistle.
Jon stands up and moves to Emma's side. He puts his arm around her.
'Not whistling at my wife are you?' he calls out good-naturedly to the rear of the dhow, but the blonde man is out of ear shot.

Then Jon yawns again.

An hour later Emma and Ali have caught enough fish for lunch. Ali tells Emma he will continue to sail over to the island and, as he does so, Emma yawns.
'Sorry,' she says.
Ali suggests she has a sleep. Emma notices that Jon is already dozing – his cigarette has burned down next to his fingers leaving a small slug of ash next to his hand. His mouth is open. He looks comic. It makes Emma feel fond of him. She goes and lies next to him and closes her eyes, letting the sun move over every part of her body.

The next thing she knows she is woken up by sea splashing over her. The water is shockingly cold and it wakes her suddenly. She opens her eyes. Jon is not next to her. She sits up and sees that the sky is dark and it is flashing with lightning. She is shivering but she still cannot see Jon. In fact, she cannot make out anything. The boat is rocking precariously back and forth. The waves are getting bigger and bigger. Some are tipping right over the side of the boat. Emma tries to stand up but she cannot. She flails wildly around, trying to find something to steady herself on. She only has time to see Hamid's eyes staring blankly in front of her when the boat suddenly heaves to the left and buckles under a huge wave, and she is tipped in to the sea.

Down she goes, down and down in the whirlpool of the sea. The surface glints above her but it gets more and more faint and further and further away until, almost calmly, she thinks what a stupid way to die. But suddenly she starts rising again, pulled by some invisible force. She surfaces, spluttering, into what is essentially hell. There is pouring rain. The sea is churning. She can't see anything. She is not sure if she is crying or not but then... she feels an arm pulling her.

It is Jon. He yanks at her, forcing her on her back and cupping her head and his hands, and somehow he drags her to where the dhow is tossing upturned in the sea. Ali is clinging to the wreckage. He looks utterly terrified. Emma cannot tell if he is crying or whether the water on his face is rain or sea. She cannot tell if she is crying either. She can see that Jon's mouth is open. He is obviously shouting instructions to her but she cannot hear him. He pulls her to the dhow and then heaves her up on top. She is left shivering, Ali clinging on next to her as Jon disappears.

Emma is frantic. Lightning flashes everywhere. She is trying to see in the gloom but she can't make anything out. She is convinced Jon has drowned for she has not seen him for what seems like an age. This makes her panic. Jon has died. He has saved her and died. She knows she is crying now but then, suddenly, Jon appears with Hamid on his back. Hamid is screaming. Even above the noise of the storm Emma can hear the wailing that is being forced uncontrollably from his body. He is on Jon's shoulders but he is panicking, flailing around as if unaware of the man beneath him trying to save him. Jon keeps disappearing under the waves. Hamid is unwittingly killing him. Emma reaches forward to try and pull Hamid onto the boat but she cannot get him without slipping off. She inches towards him but immediately feels unsafe, as if she, too, is about to slip into the swirling sea forever.

She has to make a split decision – to grab Hamid and possibly risk herself or to stay rooted to the spot. She finds she cannot move any further towards Hamid. She just sits and watches as Jon keeps coming up and gulping for air and then going down again – like a drowning dog.

Then suddenly Jon reaches out one ghostly arm and grabs the dhow and somehow, with superhuman effort, pulls himself up, whilst getting Hamid off his shoulders and into his arms. Emma is still petrified. She cannot move. They look like some ghastly depiction of a journey to Hades – wailing, drowning souls condemned to death.

Emma doesn't know how long they stay like this for. By the time they are rescued, when the storm has passed, she feels as if she has been made of starch. Her tongue is swollen. Her limbs are encrusted with salt. She can barely move any part of her body. She feels herself being dragged into another dhow. She lies on the floor remembering how Hamid slipped from Jon's arms again and again and how Jon had found him again and held him up so desperately, silently begging for help, help Emma did not give him. She can hear the chatter as the men help the four survivors into the rescue dhow. She can hear Ali sobbing. She can feel Hamid staring at her. She closes her eyes. But then she feels a body next to her. She can smell him. He slips a hand in hers and squeezes it as the tears fall finally down her face.
'Mrs Carrington,' is what he says.

December | Stockholm
Miranda Glover

Johanna and her children are buffeted towards the jetty by a cold wind as the ferry lurches in. The queue isn't long and Magnus and Katharina hop on ahead of their mother. Flashing their passes, she follows them into the cabin. She no longer notices the familiar smells inside the boat; wood polish, engine oil and ground coffee. Nor the blank, morning faces of the other passengers settling down with their rustling papers for the ten-minute crossing. The children are already seated by a window at the rear. Magnus pulls a worn exercise book from his satchel and begins mouthing spellings with an earnest frown. Katharina looks vaguely from the window at swooping gulls. Johanna sits down next to her daughter as the boat shudders then bounces back out over the choppy water, engine thrumming.

Winter's finally arrived. For weeks a curdling gloom has deadened the water's reflections; this nothing season yawning its way into mid-December. Now the wind is howling through scudding clouds above the archipelago, whipping light out with its tail. Soon the heavy moisture will fall as snow and Stockholm's islands will gleam again.
"Papa's having lunch with Uncle Per," Johanna murmurs, as much to herself as to the children. "They're going to plan next summer's trip, to Ingaro."
"Cool," mumbles Magnus, eyes fixed on his exercise book. Katharina half smiles, and continues to dream.
Johanna looks from the window, lets memories of her father scatter across the rising waves. Last year they hadn't returned to the summer house. It had felt too soon. For the first time in decades, sunlight had been Ingaro's sole inhabitant. But at the weekend Johanna had told Alex, her husband, that she thought she would be ready by July, to go back.

The playground crackles with life. Hurling his satchel at a waiting bench,

Magnus becomes a plane, gliding towards a huddle of boys. Katharina hangs back with Johanna, then, spying her friend Micha, flutters her fingers and grins. Micha skips towards them, her legs suddenly long and gangling. The girls link arms and their heads come together. Confidences mix. Johanna spins back to the moment her waters with Katharina broke, like a plug pulled out. A warm gush had drained between her legs and across the cobbles at Gamla Stan. And then the first intense contraction. Ten whole years ago.

"Hi, Johanna, good weekend?"
She refocuses, blinks and engages with a pair of concerned, dark eyes. Known eyes. Eyes that absorb her. She'd like to look away but it's impossible. Instead her mouth opens and truth spills out.
"They look so independent. It left me reeling."
Micha's dad throws Johanna a smile that turns her face bright. The grey prickles on his unshaved chin sparkle like frost. He is wearing a khaki coat with fur around the hood. It masks his hair.
"Growing too fast, I know," he says. "But it's good to be aware of it, to hold the images in your mind."

Erik always takes Micha to school. And Johanna always sees him. Today he's wearing his customary paint-stained jeans and heavy leather boots. He knocks his feet together to keep them warm. His hands are shoved inside his deep coat pockets.

Alex never brings the children to school. Leaves at six every morning, in the dark, to go to the city. Today he is to have lunch with Per. Her husband and her brother, best friends, colleagues on the stock market and brothers-in-law. Talking about a shared holiday at the family summerhouse, but this time without the patriarch; without Fredrik. All three cut from the same city cloth. Pressed cotton shirts, cashmere mix suits, tan leather brogues. Clean fingernails. Generous to a fault. It's what she knows; where she comes from. East Stockholm with its high-ceilinged apartments, creaking wrought iron lifts, thick carpets that mute dinner party conversations to a soft hum.

"The studio's like ice," he says. "I need gas."

"Do you want a hand?"

She doesn't know why she said it.

"If you have time, sure."

His face masks any sense of surprise.

"I'm meeting my stepmother," she says hurriedly, "for lunch at the Grand. So I have a couple of empty hours."

"Ah, Helena," he says. "Of course."

The playground has emptied. They fall into step, turn and leave together. His pace is equal to hers. His shoulders in line with hers. His eyes look forward with hers. Silence sits around their shoulders like a blanket. And the air no longer feels cold.

First they get coffee. It's a small cafe on the corner. Wooden tables, tea lights, licking small flames inside glass holders, elephants walking in tail-linked lines around the walls. The owner is neat-faced, has severely cropped grey hair, crimson lips. She wears a black sweater, and a pair of gold glasses hang from colourful beads around her neck. She puts them on and beams at Erik, and then at Johanna.

"Micha left her book," she says and reaches for it from under the counter.

"We've been coming here for years," Erik tells Johanna as they sit. "Since Lotta and I broke up, it's where we switch Micha over. We always have a coffee, Micha a cocoa, the three of us, like a family. Micha loves that."

"A third home," says Johanna.

Erik's eyes keep hold of hers. He has a ring on his left index finger. Gold with a deep red stone.

"Exactly," he says. "Away from each of our own."

Until now their exchanges have kept them in the playground. A sentence here, another there. In the beginning, normal sentences. "Did Micha mention the ice-skating party?" "Are you aware of the music practice on Thursday?" "How did Katharina do in the test?" More lately, the start of speaking from within.

The woman brings tall glasses filled with warm, milky coffee and a basket of muffins which they had not ordered.

"A small offering," she says. "It's not often that Erik brings a friend."
A friend. Johanna wonders at the word.
"Did you decide, about the summer?" he asks. "Are you going to go back?"
She'd mentioned Ingaro last week in the playground. Her father's sacred
retreat, the summerhouse of her childhood.
"Yes," she says. "It's the next big step."
"You look tired today," he adds.
"I slept badly."
"Maybe you need to go back to bed?"
"I'd feel guilty."
"It's good to break your own rules sometimes. Guilt's a useless emotion.
Achieves nothing."
"Like jealousy?"
"Maybe the two are connected, yes. What made you think of jealousy?"
The words slip easily between them, like currents in a stream. To her
surprise, an image of Helena swims behind Johanna's eyes.
"No idea," she lies.
Erik's creasing eyes reveal his curiosity. She blushes like a child. They
return to their coffee, and when they're done, he gets up to pay.

They get gas from the hardware store two blocks away. It is a large blue
cylinder and the owner lends Erik a metal trolley to wheel it down the
road.
"You really didn't need my help," says Johanna.
Erik shrugs, "Guess not, but why don't you come back to the studio
anyway? It's only a block away. I'm working on a series of Micha. I'd value
your opinion."

Erik has a reputation. His portraits are shown in the Museet Moderna
in the city. He's won the National Contemporary Swedish Art Award,
twice. His work pushes boundaries, often uses mixed media. Oil and
shattered porcelain or driftwood smoothed by the Baltic Sea. Johanna
knows his art both from the museum and from her father's apartment
walls. It is what first took them to a new level, in the playground, when
she told him.
"I thought I knew your face," he'd exclaimed. "I painted you father, then
his wife, Helena, twice. She was wonderful, so conscious."

"Conscious?"

"There's a certain bond that grows, you know," he'd said, "between artist and sitter. She was knowing, like your father, insightful. I liked them both, very much. How are they now?"

He hadn't heard, until then, of her father's death.

Erik stops outside an old warehouse building, presses a code and shoves his weight against the wooden door. She helps him lift the trolley over the threshold into a reclamation yard.

"There, you see, I did need you after all," he says.

He's teasing her. It feels wrong. She can't help but like it.

"Used to be a fruit warehouse," he explains as together they drag the trolley across the cobbles, past old wooden boxes and redundant palettes, piled high. There's no sign of life.

"This way."

He leads her to a goods lift to the left of the yard, closed by a heavy metal gate, turns a key and opens it up. Then, together, they pull the gas canister inside. He draws the metal doors closed behind them. There is a dim emergency bulb but otherwise it is shadowy inside. The lift groans and clanks slowly as it rises two floors. There is not a lot of space between them. She can feel him breathing near her skin. Warm, sweet breath.

The studio's a large, narrow room, with two long windows to one side. The new winter sun streams into the space, throwing the dust in the air into relief, like the tiny bugs you see over the water at Ingaro. Erik immediately pulls the gas towards a large heater and begins to disconnect the empty canister. It smells like the art rooms when she was at school, of linseed oil, paints and turpentine, charcoal dust. Dry.

Exposed beams run above their heads. The window-free walls are loaded with shelves, stacked with paints and tools, pieces of wood and boxes. Below them canvases are stacked in a series of racks. A large easel dominates the centre of the room. Next to it there's a long table where paints and brushes are set out in neat lines. In the near corner there's a bed covered with a deep, red cover, piled high with cushions. Beside it, a large reading lamp and a bookshelf laden with books and catalogues. A pair of reading glasses sit next to the bed on the floor, on top of a thick book. On its cover Johanna can make out the single word 'moderna'.

She hears a hiss and a click, then the sound of gas igniting. Erik stands up and rubs his hands together.
"So, this is me," he says. "Do you want to take a closer look?"
She moves across the space and stands next to him, before the large portrait on the easel. An emerging image of Micha on a beach; opalescent skin, long, dark hair curling down her back. She's wearing rolled up jeans, a red T-shirt. Her eyes look down at bare feet, painted onto real sand, mixed into the oil so it shimmers. She's holding a large, shiny, silver fish. Behind her are the sparkling waters of the archipelago.
"It's the sixth in a series."
He's standing so close that she feels his elbow brush her arm, even through their thick coats.
"Each represents a stage in her childhood. This is now. I feel her slipping away from me, ready to swim away. Let me show you the rest."

Erik strides to the other side of the studio through a stream of light. His hood is now down and his hair glimmers; the same dark, curling hair as his daughter's, but flecked with grey. He is tall and agile. He pulls one, then another and another canvas out from the racks. Soon five are propped up against the studio wall. In each, Micha appears at a different stage of childhood, a range of objects in her hands; a duck, a porcelain doll, a piece of wood shaped like a spoon, a gold crown studded with jewels, a garden fork with a small blue bird perched on its handle. Always the same translucent light, the same brown eyes gazing at bare feet. They are compelling, detailed portraits, like Renaissance paintings, but impasted with shells and stones and real gems and sand and fabric and gold. Timeless and still.

"I'll make us tea," he says, then points to the bed. "Sorry, that's my only chair. When you've done with looking you could take a rest while I get to work."
"I'm sorry. Should I go?"
"No, please, don't go. I feel ready to get started and that's unusual."
Erik moves to a small kitchenette in the far corner and puts a kettle on

the stove, then he moves to the easel and begins to fiddle with paints and brushes.

Please don't go. Johanna continues to absorb the pictures. Her eyes move between them, settle on details, then move on, as if exploring endless routes on a series of biographical maps. Eventually she turns from them and watches him. He's still wearing his coat; applying paint to the canvas, eyes fixed in concentration.

First Johanna sits down on the bed, then she leans back against the cushions. After a while Erik moves back to the stove, prepares, then brings her tea. Standing next to the bed, he unzips then removes his coat. Underneath he's wearing a dark green sweatshirt, zipped up to his neck. He observes her watching him. Then he smiles, slowly turns and puts the coat on a hook hanging from one of the beams, and rubs his hands together.
"Getting a little warmer," he says, and moves back to his easel.

"Micha's changed in so many ways and yet not at all," he tells her as he picks up his brush and begins to paint again. "When Lotta gave birth to her we were living in San Diego. She was teaching for a semester, at the university. It was intensely hot. We had a beach house and when Micha slept, I painted. When she woke, I cared for her. I remember thinking that the light was too intense, that she needed to be protected from its rays; she was so small and fragile, had her own inner-brightness that illuminated. She didn't need the sun to make her shine. It was a relief to bring her home to Stockholm, our shadowland. It's so much kinder to all of us, at least to our skin, if not always our spirits."

"I love it when Micha's here. She stretches herself across the bed like a cat – reads or chatters or quietly watches me work. She loves to sing, to draw. Sometimes she simply curls up and dreams. She doesn't really seem to need anyone else, rarely demands to see a friend. Apart from, recently, she often talks about Katharina."
Johanna's been drifting, rouses to the mention of her daughter.
"She's becoming important to Katharina's sense of herself, too," she replies slowly. "I think they test out their feelings and opinions on one another."

"Like a precursor to their first lovers," says Erik.

Lovers. She finds no words for response. Instead Johanna leans back against the cushions and her mind moves to last night. As Alex had made love to her a jumble of distant memories had flickered through her mind. Ingarö: Katharina no more than a few weeks old. Magnus, a toddling infant, paddling in the shallows. Katharina screeching then sleeping in the shade of the birch trees. Plastic toys strewn across the summerhouse floor. Unwashed plates. Toast crumbs on the table. Smeared blueberry juice across Magnus's mouth. Piercing light streaming in like an accusation over their domestic chaos. The tick, tick tock of the old white clock. The thick, sweet scent of elderflower, its pollen falling over the mantelpiece like dust. Damp evening air, creeping in through the windows from the forest. The making and remaking of love on unmade sheets in the midnight light. Bone aching, exhilarating fatigue.

Last night it had not been like that. Sex was still regular, but had become tinged with anxiety – at something lost. When Alex finally rolled away from her, Johanna had lain in the dark for hours and listened to him sleep; tried to figure out what it was. That is why today, she felt so incredibly..
"Tell me more about your father's death," says Erik, "I remember him so clearly."
"It was just over a year ago," she says. "His funeral was held on a cruelly cold Wednesday morning."
"Like today?"
"Yes, just like today."

Johanna misses her father's ability to see through her vacant gazes. Fredrik knew how to pull her back out. Without him a part of her seems to have lost the will to speak. Not to analytical, caring, consistent Alex, nor to Per – kind, generous Per. Definitely not to Helena. Not to anyone, until perhaps now. Suddenly it feels imperative. To get it out. She takes a sip of tea.
"I see images of that day almost as if they're through smeared windows," she says. "Many men there, men in dark, formal suits, powerful, nameless men from corporations. His daytime people. Women too, of course; pretty, neat women from the office with composed faces; and a couple

of more glamourous ones, who wept silently but who no one knew. Neither attended the gathering afterwards. None of it had anything to do with me, with us."

Erik's stopped painting. He's looking across at her, brush held up in his hand.

"How's Helena doing?" he asks.

"She's tidy in her grief, as in all other aspects of her life," Johanna replies. "Didn't let her guard down. Performed as if she were hosting yet another drinks party for some of her husband's more significant business associates. She has it down to a fine art; the light chit-chat, the ability to raise her eyes just above the level of the person she's speaking to when it's time to move on, the flicker of her lashes towards the waitresses when a glass needs refilling. It wasn't until afterwards that she vanished. Three months passed and no one saw her."

"Are you friends?"

Johanna thinks.

"We meet once a month," she says. "Today's the day, always at the Grand. I don't like to go back to the apartment. I don't really feel we have anything to say to one another. My father was our only common ground. Without him there are only memories."

Erik puts the brush down. Slowly moves across the space and sits down next to her on the bed.

"When did they marry?"

"I was twenty-one. I'd lost my own mother at eighteen. I felt I had no use of another."

"We all need different things at different stages in our lives," he says. Then he leans towards her, very gently takes a strand of her hair and tucks it behind her ear.

"Your colouring is unusual for a Swedish woman," he says. His voice is very quiet. He's scrutinising her face. "And your hair, copper-coloured and so very fine. Your father had the same extraordinary hair and sea–green eyes.

I liked painting him. I'd like to paint you, too, one day, if I may."

Johanna cannot move. She wants to kiss his beautiful lips. She wants to undo his clothes, to rub his warm flesh against hers. She wants him

177

so badly she thinks she might die if he doesn't take hold of her, undress her, occupy her. But Erik does not touch her and she does not move any closer towards him. They simply sit and fill each other with their eyes. Eventually he grins, gets up and moves back to his canvas. She finishes her tea with trembling hands, then gets up off the bed, buttons up her coat.

"I really must go," she murmurs. Her voice sounds hollow and distant, not like her own. "I don't know where the time's gone. I'm going to be horribly late."
He puts down his brush once more, moves towards Johanna and kisses her lightly on the cheek.
"Think about my proposition," he says.

The city outside seems bitter cold and bright and loud. Birds shriek, cranes clank, cars thunder. The air tastes of salt from the sea and parches her tongue. She walks purposefully across the bridges and down the narrow lanes she knows so well. Then out into the harbour, lined with its tall, pale, stoic buildings, the air here tinged with the stench of engine oil, the ferries coming and going across the turbulent waters. As she turns towards the Grand Hotel, majestic and glittering on the far side, she feels the first flurries of snow.

Helena's already sitting in one of the blue velvet armchairs in the quiet tea-room, overlooking the greying harbour. A glass of water is set before her and she's holding the lunch menu in her fine hand. She looks a little frail, like a starling, Johanna thinks, yet beautifully composed.
"Come and sit down," Helena urges. "My dear, you look a little. flushed."
"I rushed," says Johanna, "I... I was with that artist, you know, Erik Jansen, who painted you and Papa; his daughter's friends at school, with Katharina."
A moment's interest passes Helena's face. Then she looks back down at the menu. Johanna wonders what of her morning, she is displaying in her eyes. They have never been able to lie. Lunch passes in a haze of small talk but she can't concentrate on anything but the sensation of Erik's hand placing the strand of her hair behind her ear. With her own hand, Johanna touches the place his fingers brushed her skin.

Finally, the meal is finished.

"Would you like coffee?" the waitress asks.

Johanna thinks of Erik's portraits, hanging on her father's apartment walls.

"Can we have it at home?" she asks.

"Of course, darling," Helena replies.

They take a cab through the city, now cowering under a thick storm of snow. People hurry along the pavements, shoulders huddled. Street lamps flicker and light in response to the mid-afternoon dusk. The car pulls up outside an imposing, nineteenth century apartment block and they make their way in. Slowly mount the stone stairs. Helena turn the key in the apartment's heavy door as Johanna stands aside. The home of her childhood, the place where her mother and her father and Per and she had lived and loved. The place where, later, Fredrik and Helena had lived and loved. Then she crosses the threshold. Inside she smells the deep, familiar scent of lavender and polish and expensive fabrics. The thick silence of wealth. For a moment Johanna shuts her eyes and breathes it in.

They enter the drawing room and Johanna sits down on the large sofa opposite the fireplace as Helena disappears. There it is, above the mantelpiece: Erik's portrait of her father, painted in his prime. He's standing in his office, by the window. Painted to scale. Life-size. It's a great portrait, a commissioned portrait. It highlights his green, penetrating eyes, his copper hair.

"I still love to look at it," says Helena from the door. "Erik's a wonderful artist, he sees straight into the soul."

"Where are his portraits of you?" asks Johanna. "They've gone."

"Oh, I had them taken down, put into storage," Helena replies, too dismissively.

Johanna turns and observes her stepmother. A very faint flush has reached her cheeks.

"Why?" she asks. "He was talking of them today, of how pleased he was with them, with you."

"Maybe he sees too much," Helena replies, hurriedly.

"Too much?"

Now Helena hesitates.

"Like a magpie; he steals you. Your emotions. It can be disarming to be captured like that, to be so readily understood."

"Maybe it's a rare talent."

Helena looks weary. The radiating light with which she used to control a room has left her.

"Of course it is," she says it carefully as she moves into the room and stands next to Johanna. Together they observe the portrait of Fredrik. "And one to be used with great care. With someone like Freddie, it's fine. Look at him there; strong and confident and full of wisdom. But when I look at Erik's paintings of me, it's like looking into a mirror that cannot lie. I was too transparent. He painted my shadows as well as my light."

"You looked beautiful in them, Helena," says Johanna. "And you still are. Actually, he asked to paint me."

"He did?"

"Yes, I'm not sure. What do you think?"

"Just be careful, Johanna," Helena replies. She looks troubled. "Such a talent requires a scaringly rational eye and, perhaps, an unusually cold heart. It might be too soon, you know, since your father. I worry you might feel..." she searches for the right word but Johanna thinks she's found it first. It's what made her flee from the studio this morning. At the time she thought she had liked the sensation. Now, listening to Helena, she's no longer sure.

"Exposed?"

"Exactly. Exposed. You have to be strong enough to allow that to happen. Now, on to more exciting things."

Until now Johanna had not noticed that in her hands Helena's been holding a small green box.

"I've been waiting for the right moment, to give you this," she says. "I think it's now, a year on. And I have something to tell you too."

Johanna takes and opens the box. Inside is her stepmother's engagement ring. Johanna remembers the day Fredrik gave it to Helena. How the sight of it on her finger had stung.

"I could have had it made smaller," she says, "but my fingers are so frail these days, they can hardly withstand the weight of the rock!"

Johanna takes the sparkling diamond from its box and holds it in her palm.

"I know you miss your mother dreadfully and that Freddie always fulfilled all the parental roles you could possibly have needed. And goodness me, now you're nearly 40 – a mother yourself, you have little need for one of your own but."

"Thank you," interrupts Johanna.

As she slips the ring on to her left index finger her mind flickers once more to the unknown women who had attended the funeral, and then to the moment this morning, on the bed, with Erik, when she had felt such irrational desire; such acute need.

"He's bequeathed you and Per the summerhouse," Helena carries on, hesitantly. "I haven't been able to give it up until now – leaving it will be like leaving the centre our our life together, it was the key to his spirit, the place where he was unconstructed; away from the city, the financiers, the business of his life, the other... distractions. Actually it's where I went after he died. Just wandered from room to room throughout the winter, as the wind howled outside."

Generally Helena is a woman of few words. Now they spill from her like water. As she listens, Johanna sees it. The fragile look she now remembers in Erik's paintings of her stepmother, before she knew how to read them. It was that same fragility that made Helena beautiful. It was a fragility she knew she now felt herself.

"I think you're right, Helena," she says, "I'll turn Erik's offer to paint me down, at least for now."

As she turns her finger to the light and watches the diamond gleam, Johanna's mind moves to Alex. Calm, caring Alex. Alex who loved her. Alex who would never be able to see into that core in her, but who would always protect her, give her the armour she needed, in life, in order to survive it.

"We must all go to Ingaro together, this summer," she announces spiritedly. "We'll take Papa's favourite walks, tell all the tales we can remember about him, maybe even write them down. And in the evenings, once the children are in bed, we could sit in the garden and talk, about the family, about the future."

"I'd like that," replies Helena with a startling new energy. "Yes, Johanna, I'd like that very much."

About the writers – and their choice of item to put in the suitcase

Lucy Cavendish

I am a journalist and author and these are the first short stories I have written. I work mainly for *The Sunday Telegraph, The Observer, The Times* and *The Daily Mail*. I also contribute regularly to women's magazines. My first two novels, *Samantha Smythe's Modern Family Journal* and *Lost and Found* are published by Penguin. My third, also to be published by Penguin, *A Storm in a Teacup,* will be out in April, 2010. I am currently working on a fourth novel and a novella which has lots of sex in it. I live beneath a set of melancholic hills with my (rather jolly) partner and (very naughty) four children, plus the many animals we keep on acquiring.

In the suitcase I will take a photograph of me and my eldest son because it made me laugh at a time when my heart was broken.

Miranda Glover

I am a mum, novelist and magazine editor. My husband is a photographer. Between us we have two very cool kids and a mad black dog. I have published three novels with Transworld; *Meanwhile Street* (Sept 2009) about contemporary life in West London, *Soulmates* (2007) about nature, nurture and raising twins and *Masterpiece* (2005) about an identity-shifting performance artist. I am currently researching two new novels, one set in Italy in 1908, the other about small-town England today.

In the suitcase I will take my cheap and tacky lilac phone because I would feel lost without it.

Alexa Hughes Wilson

Six years ago, I packed up/in my Texas roots, New York inspirations, academic aspirations, and Seattle rain to move to South Oxfordshire with my husband, baby girl and two year old son. I now live in the countryside surrounded by horses, cows, sheep, and books. (Sadly only the latter actually belong to me!) Despite my natural disposition, I have become a fitness addict, in hopes of out-running and out-dancing the dark hounds nipping at my heels. When I do sit down, I enjoy a good laugh, a ripe mango, insane films and perhaps a glass of wine.

In the suitcase I will take my squashed and beribboned cowboy hat because my pink tutu didn't quite fit…

Rachel Jackson

The first short stories I wrote were for *The Erotic Review*, under Rowan Pelling, in 2001. It was such deliciously naughty fun that I didn't put my pen down for two years. Since then I have written for many women's magazines and been signed to Curtis Brown for a first novel. At present I live, love and write a few feet from the Thames, in a rural South Oxfordshire hamlet, with my partner and his twins. We share our life with assorted pets, much music, cherished clutter, joy and orchids and my present surroundings have inspired me as much as my Jamaican-Nigerian roots.

In the suitcase I will take my beloved red, patent, high-heeled shoes, to remind me of where I came from and where I hope I'm going.

Anne Tuite-Dalton

In the daytime, I do school runs, shopping, washing, dog walking and generally look after my three children, hens and tortoise. Early in the morning or when I can snatch one or two hours from the day, I sit down and write. Writing within the group and then for *The Leap Year* has been both exciting and fulfilling. I used to teach French and I loved that too but it seems like a lifetime ago. When I first came to Britain from the South of France in 1990, I travelled to Edinburgh on a night bus and always remember the long brownish scarf I had at the time; it was quite ugly but kept me warm and comfy on my way north. A few years ago I found a replacement:

In the suitcase I will take with me my soft and very beautiful long pink scarf.

Jennie Walmsley

I've worked for many years as a TV and radio producer – travelling the globe, pursuing pictures, sounds and facts for deadline. I recently moved with my family – partner and three kids – out of London, to chase big skies and breathe fresh air. I have taken the opportunity to shirk the limitations of journalistic integrity, and fossick around in my literary imagination.

In the suitcase I will take my identity – the perfume I've worn every day for the last twenty years.

For more information about
The Contemporary Women Writers' Club
or our new imprint, Queenbee Press,
please visit:

www.queenbee.co.uk

Lightning Source UK Ltd.
Milton Keynes UK
10 December 2009
147306UK00001B/42/P